Garbio

Stories of Chicago, its garbage, and the Dutchmen who picked it up

Chapbook Press

Chapbook Press

Chapbook Press
Schuler Books
2660 28th Street SE
Grand Rapids, MI 49512
(616) 942-7330
www.schulerbooks.com

Printed at Schuler Books in Grand Rapids, MI on the Espresso Book Machine®

Garbio: Stories of Chicago, its garbage, and the Dutchmen who picked it up

Library of Congress Control Number: 2010913723

ISBN 13: 978-1-936243-09-9
ISBN 10: 01-936243-09-1

Garbio

Stories of Chicago, its garbage, and the Dutchmen who picked it up

Foreword

In late nineteenth century Chicago, it is safe to assume that an enterprising Dutchman approached a merchant or restaurant owner with a novel idea. The Hollander would take the man's refuse ashes or garbage and, for a fee, dispose of it on his farm in the country. Thus was born the first Chicago disposal system. The Dutchman's extended family and neighbors would notice how one man's garbage can be another man's bread and butter, and in time, the ethnic Dutch in the Chicago area came to dominate the business.

"Picking up" seemed to fit the Dutch temperament. Over the years more than four hundred Dutch-owned refuse companies operated in the Chicago area, manned by thousands of drivers and helpers. They proudly call themselves "Garbios." The origin of the word is lost in the dim past, but it likely was a "spin-off" of the Italian word Mafioso who lived check by jowl with the Hollanders.

It began in the 1880s when fresh immigrants from the northern Netherlands province of Groningen, who settled on the city's West Side, found work as "night scavengers" picking up cinders and refuse. This was hard, dirty work fit only for "greenies." But it suited the Dutch well. They had come off the farm in the Old Country and were determined in America to "be their own boss." And they loved to work with horses. For $200 they could buy a horse and a wagon and begin picking up for $2 a load. They never lacked for work, even during the Great Depression. Their favorite adage was: "Your garbage is our bread and butter."

By the 1930s, the Dutch controlled the garbage industry in Chicago and owned many of the dumps. The instrument of control was an owner's group formed in the late 1920s called the Chicago Cinder and Scavenger Truck Owners Association. Critics aptly named it the "Dutch Mafia;" members referred to it simply as "The Association."

Working the city streets and alleys in the wee hours of the morning, garbios faced every form of lowlife—drunks, prostitutes, corrupt cops, union goons, mobsters, and yes, RATS as big as cats. And serious injury was only a misstep away. Statistics show that refuse hauling has been one of the more dangerous jobs in America.

The men developed a special camaraderie that came from the loneliness of the night, the smelly cans they had to "hump" and dump, and the ethno-religious bond they shared. They lived together in dense Dutch neighborhoods, talked after work on the front porches, worshipped together in the Dutch Reformed churches, and even lived out their days in church-affiliated retirement homes. Garbage was on their tongues morning to night seven days a week.

The garbios began with horses, went to trucks (often reluctantly) in the 1920s, and then in the 1950s to power packer trucks, "Dempster Dumpsters," and steel "roll-offs." No more aching backs. Capital, not labor, now became a problem. Trucks with hydraulics cost ten times more than the vehicles they replaced.

But raising the needed capital offered an unexpected opportunity for the Dutch. Garbage turned into gold. In the early 1970s, the conglomerates Browning Ferris Industries (BFI) and Waste Management Incorporated (WMI) raised millions by "going public" and with the cash they went on a buying spree, offering independent scavengers up to one million dollars per route (a truck and its "stops"). The descendants of the Harm Huizenga family, who combined their several companies into one publicly traded corporation, formed WMI. Overnight, the lowly garbios had become millionaires.

Larry VanderLeest grew up in the western suburbs of Chicago, the great-grandson of immigrants. He went off to college and came back to the area to teach. But garbage was in his blood too. During summer vacations and school holidays, he drove garbage trucks in Chicagoland to make ends meet.

The stories of the garbios are out there. VanderLeest heard them growing up. Now he has written them down in his delightful style and verve. The tales capture a way of life that has disappeared but continues to fascinate young and old. Don't believe everything you read here, but relish the stories anyway. They are as true to life as a good storyteller can make them. Here fiction is truer than fact.

—Robert P. Swierenga, Author of:
Dutch Chicago: A History of the Hollanders in the Windy City (2002)

Preface

A Book about Hauling Garbage?

Probably from the moment when Adam and Eve were finished eating their apple and wondered what to do with the core, we have wrestled with what to do with our refuse, how to dispose of it, where to dispose of it, when to dispose of it, and if to dispose of it. It is also true that many of us put the garbage by the street at night and our concern about it ends immediately. Soup cans, steak bones, paper napkins, roofing shingles, grass clippings, and worn out mufflers all magically disappear. One might also speculate on the many valuables such as gold jewelry, silverware, diamond rings, and coins that find their way into the garbage heap.

On any given day in an average landfill operation, hundreds of garbage trucks come in full and leave empty, and the wealth of our nation is evidenced by its ever-rising mountains of solid waste. Science teachers assure us that a good portion of the nasty stuff will, in time, become soil, returning some day as crops, grass, or flowers. Others warn that some substances will remain in the earth for eons, and even more ominously, that some chemicals may haunt future societies.

We have improved greatly in managing society's waste from a generation or two ago. Government regulations, a new sense of environmental awareness on the part of all of us, and improved methods in the waste management industry, combine to give new hope that the waste of today and tomorrow will be even more efficiently recycled, reused, or reduced.

The business of refuse disposal in a major metropolitan area like Chicago can be fascinating. Workers in this environment see the city as few others do, as they traverse the stores of swanky uptown areas to heavy industrial regions to sections of the city where poverty and crime have eaten away at people's lives.

On warm summer nights or on cold winter days, when I was harvesting refuse deep within the bowels of Chicago and seeing the underside of the city, I often commented to the others around me that "someone ought to write this stuff down." The full-timers would only shrug their shoulders; they saw it all and were inured to it. However, I have never forgotten the images and people I encountered in the years when I worked as a *sanitation engineer,* as the sophisticates among us would say.

The garbage hauling business held a tantalizing allure for me since I first looked for a summer job in the 1960s, and indeed for years before that. I worked my way through college by laboring "on the truck." After graduation from college, I became a teacher, and with my wife expecting a child, it was economically beneficial for me to work again on the garbage truck in the summer. Thirteen years and four children later, I found myself still doing work for garbage disposal companies when teaching breaks and summer vacation allowed. This became a therapeutic respite from the classroom and allowed me to experience the blue-collar world. It also paid quite well, something that a young teacher with four rug-rats could not dismiss lightly.

Many years have passed since I last worked on the truck. Over that time, the glow of my recollections has increased as the smell, sweat, and hurts have faded. Hauling garbage has always been an arduous and somewhat dangerous occupation. They say that the business of trash collection has changed dramatically in recent years, that it has become safer, more efficient, the domain of large corporations, and some might admit, less exciting.

My goal has been to share my sense of wonderment about a service industry that is integral to modern life, yet rather unknown, and unheralded. I am deeply indebted and very thankful to Dr. Robert Swierenga for his mentoring, editing and unquestioning support as I slogged through this book. Additionally, the material he has shared with me as he gleaned information for his documentary book *Dutch Chicago* has been invaluable. Additional anecdotes have come from childhood friends John Lindemulder, John Iwema, Ed Hoogstra, Jim Brouwer, and Tom Becvar, as well as others who served their time on the truck.

I chose Paul Stoub as my illustrator partly for our common backgrounds, but more so from my admiration of his work in many publications. His suggestions and guidance have made this book a done deal. He and I clambered on old garbage trucks, visited a landfill, and ventured down Chicago alleys to get the "feel" so important for his work.

I give great thanks to Margaret Self for being my main editor. Her approach as a non-Chicagoan and non-Dutch was very useful. A note of appreciation goes to Mel Nieuwenhuis and Nieuwenhuis Disposal for their cooperation. A special word of thanks goes to Peter Huizinga. A son of the industry, Peter's interest in, and financial support for, this project has made it possible. Finally, without the unending encouragement from my wife Kathy, I would have given up years ago. Thanks, Toots!

—Larry VanderLeest

1

First Lesson

June 1966

The warm summer night was alive with the mating hum of the cicadas as their vibrating wings brought their feverish pitch higher, higher, higher, and followed by a sudden drop. This unseen but ever-present undulating sound seemed to represent the mood of the city as a kind of constant pulse, ebbing and falling and always throbbing. Though the hot sun was mercifully long gone, the temperature still hovered at 72°, and the insects in the maples, oaks, and elms seemed to verify that activity in Chicago, if not human, at least insect, continues through the night. It was close to midnight on a Sunday evening in June 1966; and aside from the cicadas, most of the residents of suburban Berwyn were asleep, resting for the busy week ahead. Except for me.

Sitting on a lawn chair in the front yard of my parents' house and waiting to be picked up so that I could begin my work on a garbage truck for the first time, I was excited, nervous, and very wet behind the ears. Here I was, seventeen years of age, just graduated from high school, needing money to begin my college education. This was to be my first real job, I considered, working full-time five days a week. Working on a garbage truck did not seem at all unusual. In fact, I assumed it was the thing to do. I was of Dutch extraction and that is what many young men in my clan did.

For vague reasons, of which I was rather ignorant at the time, the rubbish removal business in Chicago had become the domain of a small enclave of immigrants from the Netherlands. If you worked on the "truck" that was almost a mark of distinction. I did not fully learn the cultural and sociological forces that led to this phenomenon until years later.

I was aware that three of my uncles owned scavenger businesses, as did many men in the church that our family attended. The same could be said for the other Reformed churches in the area, most of which were in the southern and western suburbs. Several of my friends' fathers either worked for or owned garbage-trucking businesses. It was an understood thing.

And although every teenage boy knew that working on the truck was going to be a hard, dirty experience, it was not undesirable. The allure of the job had been much discussed among us boys. Some knew all the facts, the leaders of the businesses, the names and types of trucks used, and who owned what routes. Moreover, we could see for ourselves the rewards that some of the young men before us had acquired by working garbage on weekends or during the summer. I vividly recall John Teune, who, upon reaching his sixteenth birthday, was awarded a brand spanking new Oldsmobile Starfire, complete with a V8 engine, earned by, as the story went around school, his many days working on the truck.

Yes, I thought to myself, with the siren of cicada wings all around me, I was now to be doing a man's job. No more McDonalds making shakes for a few hours a day, no more working on an occasional basis for a friend's father at his place of business, or for a few weeks in the summer at my uncle's mobile home park. This was a real job, and as proof, I was to be paid $5.60 an hour. In 1966, this was real money. The tranquility of the night was gradually invaded by the sound of an approaching car. Bob Van Otten, my ride and coworker, was here.

The first company to hire me was Van Otten Disposal and a perfect example of the ethnic and neighborhood tie that allowed a young man like me to get into that line of work. The Van Otten Disposal Company was a small mom and pop operation. The family itself though was large, even by that generation's standards, with eight boys and three girls. The Van Otten clan lived a few blocks from my house, and one of the stalwart sons was always a fixture in the neighborhood. As little boys, we played ball, rode bikes, and hung out. When it was time for me to get broken in, Mr. John Van Otten was neighborly enough to oblige.

Though John, the father of the tribe, would still drive on occasion, sons four and five, Jake and Bob, were running the routes at this time. Three older brothers had already done their turn with Dad, and gone on to other companies and other bosses.

We had been out on the streets for three hours, and I was on a steep learning curve. Bob, the younger of the brothers and two years older than I, was driving. In my naiveté, I thought I knew the city, but the streets and neighborhoods in which we wandered turned into a maze of roads and buildings of which I had no clue.

The mechanics of the job—how to roll rather than drag a barrel, how to dump the trash out and not let the can go into the truck with it, knowing when to get out of the cab and when not to, where to go at each stop, and how to run the packing blade—were keeping me on my toes and my eyes wide open. I so wanted to do well to please my new coworker.

By 2 a.m. we had worked our way to an area of Madison Street a few blocks away from the Kennedy Expressway, directly west of downtown. In the 1960s, this part of the city was the "skid row," an aging industrial section of small businesses, whose workers fled at the close of day to their homes in the better parts of the city and suburbs. Virtually every structure in this ten-block stretch was in decrepit condition. All the buildings were barricaded, with bars and gates covering every window and doorway, many abandoned and others giving that appearance. This all gave evidence of a very unsavory neighborhood.

Though I thought the streets presented a sleazy appearance, I found the alleys even worse. Bits of paper, rags, cans, bottles, and broken pallets lay clustered about. As our truck roared through the narrow passageways, its lights shining the way, an occasional rat scurried along the side, looking for a hole to dodge into. The loading docks, filled with cans and drums of trash, dark, smelling of urine, completed the ominous picture of a zone of death or dying.

As the workers abandoned this area when the sun went down, the undesirables seem to come out of the woodwork. They were the homeless, the drunks, the mentally ill, the doped-out, and the prostitutes who frequented this community at this hour of the night.

I felt at once intimidated and exhilarated by my new surroundings. Three hours previously my environment had been that of a middle class suburb. Now I was in one of the seedier areas of the city and wondering what lay ahead.

We approached Madison Street after a stop in the alley off West 1400, where I observed a number of people grouped loosely together near a boarded up storefront, its window remains lying in shards of glass on the concrete sidewalk, bottles and cans askew in the doorway that seemed to have been closed to customers for years.

Bob could tell something was occurring that was out of the ordinary. Heading south across the intersection, he brought the truck to a halt by applying the air brakes, disappeared out his door mumbling something about "wanting to see this" and he was gone. In a flash, I was out as well, to see or hear whatever was happening.

By the time I got around the front of the cab, Bob, dressed in his usual navy blue shirt and pants, was stopped halfway in the street, directing his attention to the group only twenty feet away. As I approached, he instinctively reached out his arm as a warning to not go any further. One of the local transients was standing on the pavement, brandishing an eight-inch knife and yelling back at others standing in a semi-circle around him. He seemed in a state of complete intoxication, draped in tattered clothes, and wore facial bruises that were obvious even from several feet away. Some of the crowd had spilled onto the road and sidewalk, while two men in particular were cursing and threatening to "get him." Yet they kept their distance, and for good reason. He held the knife in his right hand and swayed back and forth.

An argument had apparently occurred among the three, which had evolved into an outright fight. The first man had pulled out his weapon, and the effect showed on the other two. One was using a T- shirt wrapped around his neck as a temporary tourniquet. In the pale, ugly light of the street lamps, I could see the deep red of blood spreading into the dirty, white cotton. With one hand on his bandage to stop the flow, he raised his other in a gesture of anger. His partner had a bloody rag around his arm as well. The knife in the first man's hand and his wild mannerisms kept them at a distance.

Bob and I had crossed over the street to get as close as we dared when a city squad car with lights flashing came to a screeching halt. Two officers, one white and one black, leaped out and, with guns drawn, approached the scene while trying to figure out what was going on.

The man with the impromptu bandaging around his neck, the one closest to having his throat slashed, explained the situation with embellishment. The two cops, seeing the accused with the weapon, moved closer. Staggering slightly, as if ready to fall forward at any moment, yet holding the blade out at arm's length, he stood fast on the pavement. With a glance to each other and a nod of the head, there was mutual understanding that this was to be the black officer's job.

With his revolver drawn and at the ready, the cop said forcefully, "Okay, guy. Put the knife down!"

In a garbled, angry tone, and pointing menacingly, the man shot out. "You come get it, copper."

"Put the blade away, buddy, and you won't get hurt," the cop demanded.

"Shit, man," he replied, waving his weapon in the air and weaving about as if ready to fall at any moment. "Ya come get it. I dare you. C'mon." It was obvious to those of us watching this spectacle that he was high on something. The officer knew he was in a delicate situation.

Several rounds of yelling, threatening, and counter-threatening followed. More brandishing of the knife. All the while, a slow, steady approach by the police officer, holding his firearm with both hands. By now, he was within ten feet.

No more than three minutes had passed from the time the policeman had arrived to his conclusion. The man could not be convinced to drop his knife, his only source of strength and defense against the bad things that happen to people like him on the streets of the city. The officer was not backing down either. For some reason, the other cop hadn't uttered a word, apparently preferring to let his partner handle the case.

The gathering had grown to a dozen or so and, after some initial expletives and suggestions, had grown quiet. The two young men from the suburbs looked upon this real life drama with eyes wide open, wondering how it would play out.

The officer may have been pondering the issues mightily, but his internal debate didn't seem to last long. He was obviously getting nowhere. The man must have been stone drunk or on some drug. There didn't seem a safe way for the cop to do what he had to do. He apparently had no mace or any other method of disarming the guy. I imagine that the officer may have questioned if this sorry excuse for humanity was worth risking putting himself in harm's way.

He made his decision. Suddenly two short bursts erupted from his revolver, and the troubled transient got it square in the chest, falling like a brick. The street fell silent.

Together the two policemen cautiously went up to the body, lying on the dirty pavement in a dirty part of the dirty city. Some of the onlookers muttered words of dismay, disgust, or finality. A few began to drift away. Bob motioned to me that we had to be on our way; there were more stops to pick up. As the officers retreated to their squad car to call whomever they call in these situations, the body lay where it fell. By now, a rivulet of blood was finding its way to the curb. Heading west on Madison, the scene grew smaller in my mirror. My summer job was turning out to be all I had expected and more.

2

Close Call

July 1966

Within weeks, I was a veteran garbageman, or at least I had learned enough to know that we had to contend with bums that frequented the same areas in which I worked in this large metropolitan city. The alleys especially were havens for the homeless. The loading docks in such places provided natural habitats. They were often poorly lighted, not patrolled by security guards, and quiet enough so a fellow could sleep securely, knowing that he wouldn't be harassed by anybody. The only people these gentlemen might meet in the dark of night were garbagemen, and we were too busy doing our thing to give the homeless man (or the occasional woman) any hassle. But a garbageman doing his thing and a transient sleeping off a heavy dose of drinking could lead to disaster. My experiences that follow could be multiplied a hundred fold for veterans of the scavenger business.

* * *

I was with John Van Otten, the old man and owner of the company, when I had my eyes opened a little wider. This was my third week on the truck and I was still learning the ropes. John had pulled our truck into the alley off State and Harrison. We worked our way down a particularly dark stretch, to an area filled with litter of all manner, decrepit-looking loading docks, piles of rags, bottles, strewn-about cardboard, and everything that humans could do to defile their environment. No doubt this building has long since been razed and the area renewed, however in 1966, this was one of the more degraded alleys of a degraded section of the city. No one went through this passageway unless he had specific business and then only quickly.

Yet, I felt comfortable riding in the cab of the old Diamond T … because I was with John. The well-worn hat on his head, the four pens stuck in his plaid shirt pocket, his slow manner of moving in and out of the cab spoke of age and security. His sons, though well experienced on the truck, were too close to my age, too young in their talk to impart the same effect. They were fast and fun and swore wonderfully well. But in the darkness of the city at 2 AM, maturity had its place. It mattered not what the loading platform may hold, what kind of garbage may be back there, or what the situation appeared to be. As long as I could stick near John, I figured I was okay.

As he backed the truck in, sliding within two inches of a rusting steel post embedded in a pitted concrete base, John was scanning both mirrors to get a better view. It's awfully dark back there, I thought, observing him out of the corner of my eye, in awe of his ability to negotiate this big rig and wondering how he could see what he was doing.

He couldn't, it seemed. Either the work-light from the truck was insufficient or some lights on the dock were missing. This tight spot, though he had probably backed in a hundred times, seemed too difficult that night. He needed help, he said. He asked me to get out and go back to direct him, to make sure of what might be in his way.

Oh great! I thought to myself. I didn't want to go back there. This alley was black as coal and the few lights on in the far away dock landing were playing eerie tricks with shadows. Strange looking heaps of unknown compositions lay in the corners, both above and on the alley surface. The dock itself, with myriad groupings of barrels, dark and foreboding recesses and openings that led to shadowy depressions promised even greater horrors. Two o'clock in the middle of the night; and I was in the ugliest, loneliest, blackest alleyway of the city. And my boss wanted me to go back there by myself. My imagination began to work. I was convinced there lay hidden one—no—probably two men with knives and broken bottles ready to slash my throat for the ten dollars in my pocket while John, my security blanket, stayed in the cab.

However, as afraid as I was of who or what might be in the recesses of the loading area, I also had to answer to the old man. I leaped out, acting as nonchalant as possible, even as I headed for the spookiest abyss in the south side of Chicago. I went halfway, and with a quick examination, retreated to the cab. "Everything's okay," I stammered, "you can back up."

For some strange reason, my assurances didn't satisfy John. Acting a little pissed off, he jumped out and went back himself. I followed, bravely now.

There on the ground, two feet out from the loading dock and buried under a pile of rags and cardboard, lay a gaunt-looking fellow, apparently just sleeping off a drinking frenzy or drug overdose. Somehow, neither the noise of the truck or the glare of the lights had managed to rouse him.

John looked at me with Dutch uncle eyes. "Dammit, Larry. Ya see this guy? Well, I didn't! Man, I would've backed right over him. That's why I sent you back here, to check things out, to guide me back in. I don't like smashing guys to a pancake when I'm doing my job. It kind of slows me down and gets on my mind, ya know."

I mumbled some kind of apology and began to climb up onto the landing, trying to turn his attention to the garbage at hand, but he wasn't done with me yet.

"If we'd a squashed him, we would be spending the rest a' the night with the police, 'splaining things and filling out papers. Next time, damn it; check everything when I tell ya to check it. It ain't a pretty sight to run over one of these guys wit' a 40,000 pound load."

With the sermon finished and with me feeling duly reprimanded, he leaned over and rather gently, I thought, picked up the limp body. With life now stirring in his legs and his eyes finally opening, the homeless man wandered off to find another spot to crash. We continued on, while visions of school yard reprimands by a teacher came flooding back to me.

* * *

It was a week later and at precisely the same location when we found the next one sleeping it off, but in a place even more precarious. This fool—it might have been the same one, came awfully close to death, and fully convinced me of the need to roust these derelicts from sleeping near garbage stops.

Jake, the older of the two Van Ottens and a giant of a man with a less than giant brain, was driving the truck on which I was riding shotgun. Brother Bob, driving their second vehicle, had communicated via radio that he was on the way to help.

Jake had a baby-like face curiously attached to a prodigious trunk of a body with a massive set of arms and legs. He talked in a high pitched voice yet, appearances aside, was usually soft-spoken. On rare occasions, his demeanor could change when life in general or the garbage truck specifically wasn't treating him well. To cope with the problems of working in such an environment, Jake had established watering stations along the route. By the time we arrived at the South State Street alley, he was halfway through his nightly intake of a shot and a beer, yet still able to do his job well, feeling quite alive as it were.

We pulled in, took a quick check—I actually looked this time—and agreed it was clear to back up and begin the loading. Bob had arrived with his truck as well, parked it down the alley a distance and joined us. The platform was filled to overflowing with barrels and cans, and lying off to the side were many, many cardboard boxes, all about six feet long, two feet wide and one foot deep. Apparently, maintenance had gone through the entire building, all ten floors, and changed about a million fluorescent light bulbs. There had to be forty or more boxes, some full of bulbs, some empty, others containing miscellaneous crap, but every box was easy for a guy to grab and toss with a quick movement.

Bob had stopped to help us, I concluded. Someone must have called ahead to inform Bob and Jake of the extra amount of garbage that night. Yet with three guys, they figured, it was no problem. We could do what we had to do quickly and be on our way. After first tackling the barrels and cans, shoving the empties off to the side, we had room to maneuver with the boxes. Within a minute or two, we got in a groove, acting like an assembly line. Bob, younger and slighter of build than Jake, was no slouch himself when it came to hustling garbage. He dragged, pushed, and slid the boxes to his brother Jake in turn throwing them in the hopper where the compacting blade would compress the refuse into the body of the truck. My job, in addition to picking up the spare litter lying on the dock floor and tossing an occasional box, was to keep running that blade as fast as possible. If we kept up a fast pace, Jake reasoned, we would get him to his next tavern/garbage stop before the 2 a.m. closing time.

Crushing hundreds and hundreds of fluorescent light bulbs in the dead of night in a South Side Chicago alley is a surreal experience. The exploding tubes, the spewing fluorescent gas, the screaming hydraulics, the diesel racing at 2000 rpms, and the compacting pressure combined to make horrific noises. Shards of glass were flying out of the hopper, and billows of dust and gas were pouring out

of any available opening in the truck body. This, all silhouetted by the work-lights of the truck against the black of the night, made it a remarkable sight. We were making our own little version of Dante's Inferno in a back alley of the city.

I still can't quite comprehend how, through all that noise, a man, sleeping in a box six feet long, two feet wide and one foot deep, could be ignorant to the danger coming closer and closer. Yet ignore it he did, and his cardboard bed almost became his cardboard coffin. As Bob handed the umpteenth box to Jake, and he, in one quick motion completed the sweep to the hopper, the man's leg protruded out of one end. Jake, in shock as much as in anger, yanked at the appendage, and out came the stunned imbecile, screaming from the rude awakening. I immediately pulled the handle to stop the blade. The 2,000-pound, five-inch thick wall of steel with 10,000 pounds of torque stopped. The diesel engine slowed to an idle. The roar of our work ceased.

Jake, totally pissed off at how close we came to cutting this man in half, pulled him out of the hopper by his hair, stood him upright on the platform and unmercifully began to deliver hell and damnation to him. He kicked him

in the ass, gave a vile imprecation or two, followed up on him, kicked again, and repeated this for a distance of twenty feet. Brother Bob even yelled for Jake to stop, which he did eventually.

Jake returned to where we stood, entranced in this human drama, red-faced as ever, with a look of anger, fear, and confusion on his face. I asked feebly, "Jake, did you have to kick the man so hard?"

The other Van Otten just gave me a stare as if to say shut your mouth or you're next. He began to throw boxes again. I turned, taking Bob's cue and Jake's place to give him a break, and we completed the tossing of boxes into the truck. We now looked at each cardboard carton with new interest.

An episode from my childhood came flooding back as I tossed the boxes. I was probably only six or seven years of age when two of my friends and I had witnessed the power of the garbage truck for the first time, placing that vehicle, and the men who worked it in a new and higher light. Biking through an alley of the Berwyn suburb we had traveled many times before, we came upon some garbagemen doing their thing. The workers were rolling and lifting and tilting and emptying and dropping and rolling the large cans back into place. The width of the vehicle and the action of the men blocked our progress through the narrow alley. We had no recourse but to stop and watch, or go back the way we came.

Being young boys and in no particular hurry, we decided to watch what these men did. The basic principle was easy for our young minds to understand. The workers put garbage in the opening in the back, and then, amidst a thunderous roar of engine power, a big wall of metal came down from somewhere, and with a mighty sound, pushed the soup cans, paper bags, and the leftover broccoli out of sight. This we had seen numerous times in half-hearted observations.

However, this day we saw something that took our collective breathes away. One man had taken a large steel drum and, for no clear reason, after emptying the contents, held it in place as the packer blade came down, smashing the steel drum flat as a pancake. He turned to us with a smile as if to say, "Look what I just did. Isn't that cool?"

This opened our eyes like nothing before. Here was something to which we could relate. Any boy loves to smash things—bugs, spiders, flowers, other kids' toys, little brothers, whatever lay before us.

But not all things were smashable, we had learned. In fact, some things were so big and strong that they did the smashing. We all knew the heft of a garbage barrel. Each of us had one or more in our backyards and often put some trash in it. As a young boy, I occasionally tried to push one over, usually crunching a toe or two in the process. Never could do. And here, before our very eyes, an object that none of us could even lift off the ground was crushed flat. I think it was that moment in time that mesmerized me and compelled me to try my hand at running such a machine.

Now, flash forward ten years or more, and I was an operator of this source of manliness and might. Cardboard boxes, light bulbs that exploded in the night, and broken down pieces of pallets were one thing. However, the flesh, bones and soul of a human, so close to being compressed to nothingness was not what I had expected. The danger of the machinery I had to control had now begun to make an impression.

While Bob and I finished the stop, Jake, settling down as quickly as he had flared up, sat on an upside-down barrel, and lit one of his Camels. We soon wrapped up our work there and headed to Jake's next stop, and a shot an' a beer near Wells and Jackson, hoping to get there just before closing.

3

The Hole in the Wall

The Van Otten Disposal Company had one peculiar stop in the 1960s that they designated the 'Hole' near Wells and Lake Streets. The place was well named—a rectangular opening in the side of an aging building facing the alley. The structure was razed years ago, replaced by a modern glass and steel structure. The demolition crew no doubt observed many a rat scurrying for cover as the bricks came down.

Deep in his heart, every garbageman harbors a hatred for those furry creatures. Garbage-haulers know that rats bite, and if bitten, a worker can have some serious consequences. Though the occasional rodent might be found in the outlying suburbs, it is in the city, with its abundant sources of food, where the carnivorous rat is in its element.

This was one of the worse stops of the Van Otten routes and it was an 'every-other-niter.' I was introduced to the Hole and its occupants on my second night on the job. We had been picking up various small stops along Lake Street—two cans of restaurant slop here, three barrels of office trash there—and so it made no sense for the helper, which was my official title, to get in and out of the cab. Instead, I hung on to the back of the truck. This convenient method of travel from stop to stop was an enjoyable way of moving about the city, especially on warm summer nights. I saw the urban jungle from a unique perspective back there. I was acutely aware of the smells, sounds, and sights as I journeyed up and down the avenues and alleys, with my feet planted firmly on the steel platforms mounted on each side, like mini-running boards, and the truck as my chariot.

This practice is now illegal or perhaps the insurance companies won't allow it, and I guess that's one more way the job just ain't what it used to be.

My first visit to the Hole was, as usual, a learning experience. Turning down an alley, we came upon this imposing wall of concrete block and dark brick, about eight floors high. As Jake Van Otten slowed the rig to a crawl, I scanned the area for any cans, barrels, or Dumpster boxes along the side of the alley or perhaps on a loading dock nearby. We were now virtually stopped and yet there was no garbage in sight. I did notice, however, this peculiar rectangular opening in the wall, six feet high and just out of reach of anyone on the ground, a doorway without a door and no steps leading to it. Jake pulled forward in preparation for backing up.

It became clear that this strange cavity was our destination.

As the truck slowly reversed, it also became evident how I was to get into the six-foot high opening. Our truck was to be a stepladder of sorts. Jake eased the rig to within inches of the concrete barrier alongside the base of the building, the air brakes screeched on and my next lesson in 'garbology' was on the board. Here I was, eye level to a black notch in a wall, it was four in the morning in a lonely alley in downtown Chicago, and I had a premonition of what was next. Jake came around from the front and said, "OK, Larry, climb in."

I had no idea what lie in wait for me in that chamber of horrors, but my imagination was working overtime. "Jake," I murmured, "wa- what's in there?" I thought further, harder. "Who- who's in there? Any bums?"

He just smiled with a big, condescending smirk at my obvious fright, though I thought I was putting on a good bluff. "Nah, we've never seen any in there, not for a long time. The rats always keep 'em away."

I blanched. A reassuring thought.

Jake continued, "Go ahead, climb in. I'll be right behind you."

Give the man credit; he was true to his word. I worked my way up into the dark opening and fiddled around for a light, expecting to find a pull string in the air or switch along the wall. I found nothing. As I searched for the mythical illumination, Jake, joining me in this cave-like setting, affirmed my concern.

"You won't find a light in here, Lar." He grinned. "It's been out for months."

He fumbled along the side of the wall and produced a worn 4 x 8 sheet of plywood, caked with a rich menu of old, ancient and fossilized remnants of garbage. Jake deftly stuck it out through the opening as if he had done this hundreds of times and positioned the board as a kind of chute upon which we were apparently to slide the garbage down from our six-foot high perch. As my eyes adapted to the dark surroundings, I could make out ten to fifteen 55-gallon barrels and several GI cans, all filled with bottles, soup cans, paper, and assorted restaurant refuse. There were the ever-present cardboard boxes, some flattened, some not. As my eyes became accustomed to the dark, the walls were now faintly visible and the size of the Hole became evident. It appeared to be a storage area with doors leading off in three or four directions, all locked, of course. This seemed to be a common storeroom for garbage of several small businesses, at least one of which had to be a small diner.

Jake explained the procedure as he positioned the plywood sheet. "Lar, you just roll the full ones to me, I'll dump them. Stack the empties along the wall. I'll let you do the boxes."

I was agreeable. I grabbed a barrel and tipped it at an angle as the first step in rolling it over to the opening. Immediately, a rat jumped up and out of the barrel. I abandoned the container like a hot potato, let out a string of obscenities, and interjected somewhere in there the word 'rat.' I heard a deep chuckle from Jake.

"Didn't I tell ya the rats keep the bums away? This place is always crawling with 'em. Kick the barrels before you grab 'em. That'll shoo 'em away."

An excellent plan, I thought. I began to 'whale' on the barrels and drums mercilessly until they started to bleed garbage and my foot grew sore. In the blackness, surrounded by the commotion I was making, I had no idea if I was scaring away the hairy little critters or just waking up the city.

Jake looked at me with a look of exasperation on his face. "Lar—just once or twice will do. Now come on. I need 'em here."

I struggled mightily to roll one over to him and, though it had to weigh a hundred pounds if it weighed an ounce, he picked up it up as it were a kitchen wastebasket, emptying the entire contents in seconds. This display of Herculean strength, not to mention his complete fearlessness of rats so impressed me that, rather than rolling the next barrel in position, I froze, watching in awe. Jake finished with a flourish and turned to find me staring at him. With no barrel in hand, I might add.

"Hey, asshole. Roll me another one."

I was not yet the most skilled at this job.

* * *

Two nights later, I returned to the Hole. That time and throughout the summer, the ritual was the same. The truck would back up to within inches of the wall; we would climb up into the dark and fumble around for the containers. Almost every night we would hear a skittering and plopping of bushy little bodies jumping for safety as we, the big scary garbagemen came to mess up their dinnertime. I learned to kick each barrel twice, once at the bottom, once at the top. That was my signal to the rats; their table setting was closed and it was time to move on.

It was always oppressively dark in the Hole, leaving me to wonder what the floor, walls, and ceiling really looked like. I had to feel more than see my way around, always sensing that as I worked I had an audience of rats watching my every move. Yet, I learned to have less fear of the animals with each passing day. That was presumptuous of me.

One Friday night, with the weekend beckoning, partner Bob and I arrived in a lighthearted mood, attacking the refuse we met with relish. He backed the rig up; I clambered in and positioned the indestructible sheet of plywood, like always. The two of us were taking turns kicking, grabbing, rolling, lifting, and dumping.

One barrel must have had something especially delicious in it, too tempting for one stout rat to resist. I approached the drum with the usual caution, kicking it twice. Then, grabbing the edge, I tipped and began to roll the can, casually switching hands in one smooth move (I was getting good at this stuff!).

Suddenly a good-sized momma with a long tail leaped out of the barrel, possibly as shocked as I was. Losing any sense of where its safety lay, the animal ran up my arm, over my shoulder and up on to my head. I could feel its clingy feet grabbing onto my scalp and see its tail illuminated in the work light of the truck right square between my eyes as it searched for secure footing and a way out of its dangerous situation. The rat sat there for an eternity, scoping out its world from on top of Mt. Garbageman. My shouts of sheer "delight" probably didn't help any, for it finally took a leap off my head and down into the darkness. I was out of that building in a nanosecond, literally leaping for the alley, setting a record long jump that unfortunately wasn't recorded. Bob split a gut laughing and proclaimed me now a real garbio.

4

The Sewers of Chi-town

Summer 1966

Working on the Van Otten garbage truck meant that we had many restaurants to pick up. It was inevitable that we could expect soupy, lettucy, meat-greasy, apple-saucy garbage. There seemed to be a principle when it came to the type of garbage a restaurant produced. The higher-class establishments, like Berghoffs, George Diamonds, and Jimmy Wongs, had barrels and cans heavy with vast amounts of uneaten food. It seemed logical that only the rich could afford to toss such large amounts of food. Accordingly, these higher-class restaurant stops also produced the larger rats of the city as well.

However, the sloppy-spoon eateries had the wettest garbage, with what appeared to be 50 percent soup in their drums. After several of these stops, our truck would be noticeably heavier, with gallons of garbage truck stew sloshing around in the hopper. One method to absorb the excess moisture was to schedule some dry stops in between. After picking up a few office buildings producing paper rubbish or certain wholesalers that tossed large amounts of cardboard, the slop would be somewhat absorbed. However by the late 1960s it seemed these more desirable customers had been taken by the bigger scavengers and Van Otten Disposal was relegated to taking the 'messies' others didn't want.

If the garbage was excessively wet that night, by mid-morning our rig would turn into a soup can on wheels. As we traveled the downtown streets, with me hanging on the side of the truck or straddling the stew-filled hopper, it was a contest in knowing when to jump to avoid the next wave. Turning corners or coming to quick stops caused swells of a foul-smelling concoction to pour onto the ground and splash passing cars or pedestrians. The truck left its signature in alleys and the loading areas by depositing puddles of wet waste. As self-respecting garbagemen, we were embarrassed by the whitecaps in the hopper. Any police officer seeing our truck applying a coat of goulash to the streets would nail us for sure. Even fellow scavengers were bemused by our sloppy trails. But what to do?

Jake, the driver with the incurable taste for a shot an' a beer, developed a cure. He had a drainpipe installed into the bottom of the truck's body with a cap that we could open or close. Officially, this outlet was intended for use only in the landfill. However, Jake was eminently practical in that, if something needed to be done, he would do it, come hell or high water. And we had high water, or some form of it in our truck after stops like The Knife & Fork or Joe's Quick Coffee.

During the summer when I worked for Van Otten, we stopped to let our truck take a pee at least twice weekly. As the vehicle began dripping its load on Randolph or Adams Streets, we knew it was time to empty the hold. Our usual procedure was to drop down onto the Kennedy Expressway, head north, and go right back up the Monroe or Lake Street ramps. We would then stop halfway on the shoulder of the ramp, putting us at about a seven-degree angle. Jake would make sure the rig was positioned right over a sewer opening. There, pretending

our truck had some kind of mechanical troubles, we would stand by the back of the truck, discussing philosophy while we let the rig empty its bladder.

Jake would crawl under the truck and locate the capped drainpipe positioned a foot in front of the dual wheels. As I kept an eye on the streets to make sure no officers were in sight, he would unscrew the cap. Yesterday's soup and gravy, some foul concoction from that last factory and other wastewater would go gushing into the storm drain on the side of the ramp and into the system. In a few minutes our torrent of putrid garbage stew would be a dribble; we would put the cap back on and be on our way.

Now, what was the impact of that to the sewer system of the city? Were we committing some sins of environmental pollution or could the metropolitan waste department in the 1960s handle the fraction of effluent that we put in to it? I honestly don't believe we even felt the need to rationalize our actions. In our ignorance, we saw the solution into which we could alleviate our problem. We had the option to either spread the load of yuck on the streets and alleys for all to see and smell, or deposit it directly into the sewers into which it would eventually arrive. We simply sped the process along.

The scavengers of that era were often faced with such conundrums. They were asked to remove the unwanted leftovers of society. Their customers cared not what happened after it left their loading dock or alley. That was the garbageman's problem. Only a few figured it was the earth's problem. The environmental movement was the impetus to force all concerned—the producers, the governments, the removers, and the acceptors—to work together to find solutions.

5

On to Greener Pastures

1967

After one summer as a helper on a downtown garbage route, I was ready to move on. The following season offered several opportunities, but a day job working with two friends for a disposal company in the suburbs looked the most attractive.

I quickly discovered the differences between commercial and residential work. The worker picking up industrial or retail waste in the pre-dumpster era was well served if he was a beefy chunk and of good height. A strong back and steel-tipped boots were prerequisites. Some in-city routes could be back-breakers, with 55-gallon drums that defied lifting off the ground and that, if dropped, would crush toes or mutilate fingers. Carrying barrels out of basements or down several flights of stairs was a test of the spine and spirit. Before the residential incinerator was outlawed in Chicago, ash was a common ingredient in city trash. If the residue was wet, the weight would be horrendous; if dry, we were warned, be careful—the ash might be still hot enough to cause a fire in your truck.

Wrestling the barrels down the alleyway, or up into the rear hopper of the truck was an art that one had to master if you expected to last for any length of time on commercial routes. Sure—brute strength could often be enough to pick the hundred plus pound weight. But veterans learned that a certain deft touch with the leg or knee did wonders for added leverage. And while dragging the barrels would never work; even rolling them, though possible, was not the best method of transporting the cans any great distance. Before the advent of the container on wheels or Dempster Dumpster, practiced garbios had to maneuver the weight to their back. The vision of a hunkered-down chap, lugging a two hundred pound steel drum on his back, through a darkened downtown alley at 3:00 a.m. says it all. This life was brutal.

House garbage was faster, lighter, and cleaner, but just as smelly. Residential work tended to be more rigorous, and most of the young men running the trucks were lithe creatures. These were aerobic exercises par none, with continual movement of the arms, hands, back and leg muscles.

My first day on the streets of a northern suburb brought arm cramps, chapped lips (I huffed and puffed) and foot calluses. By the time I arrived home, I thought I was dying. Yet I had to go out the next morning and tackle the streets again.

The second day I was a little more prepared, wearing better fitting shoes. No calluses, but the muscle cramps returned, and my lips remained cracked and raw.

Wisdom was slow in coming, but my young muscles adjusted. By the third day the upper arm cramps and sore mouth disappeared. Each day I grew stronger and, in a sense, wiser. Within a month I was able rapidly to maneuver two cans from the curb to the truck, and if the container's weight allowed, four.

Usual practice was to empty one can at a time. Using teamwork, we would toss the empty to our colleague on the side, or bring fulls into position for the driver as he came around to help. And drivers in those days consistently got out of the cab. With up to six cans per house, and the residences packed together on small lots along two-sided streets, a helper and his driver could pack major amounts of rubbish in an hour. On occasion, the helper would work his way ahead, placing the cans in the middle of the street. A good co-worker was important and made for a pleasant day.

I was proud of my ability to approach the hopper of a rear-loading packer with two full cans and, with a deft move, swing them up and, for a few seconds, hold them topsy-turvy as the contents flowed out. It was an impressive display of young male might and a tad bit of machismo. I couldn't do that trick every stop; perhaps once in a city block; or whenever I saw a girl coming down the street.

If the trucks didn't break down, the days on house garbage could be short. The policy of the companies I worked for was: *get your work done and you can go home*. If that took five or six hours, so be it. Accordingly, with a young driver and a younger helper, we would literally keep running for the duration of the day, just to proclaim to the other garbios in our garage that a) we were done, and b) we were faster.

In the 1970s, Chicago's western suburbs seemed to have a lawn-growing contest. The homeowners and lawn farmers in Du Page County were producing enormous amounts of grass. We who hustled on the streets of Lombard, Wheaton, and Elmhurst could bet our working gloves on the fact that we would find, along with one or two cans of household trash, eight or more bags of grass clippings at almost every residence.

Now I am not an expert on cattle nutrition, but the sight of bag after bag of very rich, Kelly green grass going into my truck and two hours later into the landfill seemed an anomaly. Of course, that I had to pick the heavy stuff up was a further aggravation.

When the temperature was sitting at 90 degrees and I was dragging the nine hundredth bag of grass for the day, I would ask the hot pavement the question, "Why can't someone haul this overflowing goodness of emerald nutrition to cows, perhaps only fifty miles away, who are mooing for their supper?"

Of course, economics and politics allowed people of most suburbs to put out as much as they care to, all to be hauled away to the steadily disappearing landfills. Whether you put out one can or ten, one paper bag or twenty plastic, the charge per household was the same.

Maggots are the worst thing about house garbage. The little things emit a peculiar odor. On warm, wet days we could find them at the bottom of containers in the hundreds, swimming about in their slime. There weren't many things that repelled garbios. The occasional rat or mouse was an object to chase. Broken window glass, boards with protruding nails, washing machines still containing gallons of water and, on winter days, cans with grass clippings or leaves frozen to the sides were looked upon as part of the job. We shrugged our collective shoulders and moved on. But a can that oozed maggots was the ultimate in grossing out a guy.

I learned rather quickly that the method of hauling refuse was universal. Whether it was residential garbage by the thirty-gallon can or commercial refuse by the two-yard container (an innovation of the 1960s), the type of trucks used were often the same. No doubt about it—the garbage truck is not a thing of beauty. By nature, the vehicle is a short, squat ugly creature, designed for durability and efficiency. With a profusion of hoses, cables, chains, bars and weld points in front and on the sides, and its cargo—trash—perhaps showing in the rear, these trucks were the bulldogs of the city's streets. The owner might procure a new truck, all fresh and shiny and a thing of beauty. It won't stay that way. The typical refuse rig gets scratched and dented quickly from its daily treks into the alleys and loading docks of Chicago.

And a clean garbage truck is an impossibility. Sanitary landfills, as one may conjecture, are not sanitary, in spite of the title often applied to them. After a rainy day and for several days after, the trip into the dump or transfer station would only add another layer of filth on the foulest-looking vehicle on the street. As I journeyed along the Kennedy Expressway in my twenty-five yard packer or stubby-nosed box truck in search of more trash to pick up, I was often guilty of breaking the Tenth Commandment. I coveted the sleek, aerodynamic eighteen-wheeler Kenworths and Peterbilts, glistening with chrome mud-flaps and exhaust stacks, with their three-color paint jobs and sleeper cabs. Was it true, I wondered, what I had heard from one grizzled old-timer—that the longer one worked on the truck, the more he began to resemble his rig?

As the summer drew to a close, I tossed my gloves into the hopper on the last stop on the last day in a symbolic gesture, and took off to hit the books. But the lure of the truck and need for money always beckoned me back. During my sophomore year at college, I picked up spare cash working the Thanksgiving break for the father of a friend. With that financial success in mind, I arranged to work for several days during Christmas vacation as helper to another buddy. The week of spring break found me driving for a garbio in my church.

By that next summer I had imposed upon myself a goal—to ascertain how many disposal companies I could work for before I graduated from college. Every interlude from school found me laboring for another Dutchman. When I noted that some of my friends still worked for the same employer they had three years previously, I scorned their provincialism, and a spirit of wanderlust imbedded in my psyche.

A pattern of transitory job searches was now part of my thinking. I wanted to see and to work the vast region of Chicago. This became a source of pride when I could say to other garbagemen that I had worked for so many haulers. As best I can recall I was employed by at least eleven companies, ranging from tiny single-truck outfits to one of the larger in the Chicago region. For some, I labored a summer, others, a week, or even only a day. Only one is still in existence. All the others have merged or been bought out. Some have simply faded away.

6

Let Sleeping Men Lie

1969

I pulled my International 190 down the alley behind Randolph, between State and Wabash, and took a quick visual of the loading dock. The glare of the mercury vapor lights showed the usual cans, barrels, and stacks of cardboard, though at first glance, it looked messier than normal. The homeless guys must have beaten me here, I figured, and did their shopping.

This was my third summer of working on the garbage truck and I was back in the big city, graduated to being out on the streets and alleys all alone. The year was 1969 and I was driving a route for Nick Vander Puy & Son, another of the many operators in Chicago in the 1960s. Nick's only son had died in an accident years ago and from what I recall, the old man had never quite recovered from the blow. Nick was operating two routes on the streets of Chi-town but, at the age of sixty or more, rarely came down to the garage. His horrendous habit of smoking a Lucky Strike to the end and then lighting the next one from the stub of the first was instrumental in his terrible hacking cough.

This stop on Randolph was an every-niter, a two-for-one pickup of office rubbish and slop from a small restaurant. If things were going right, I arrive between 4:30 and 5 AM. Fifteen to twenty barrels—usually easy to handle, occasionally some loose sheets of cardboard, leave a ticket under the door, and then on to the next one. Directly across the alley was the Fairmont Hotel, where on occasion, I would meet Jake Van Otten and his helper, Roger Ouwinga, from Van Otten Disposal. Rog, like me, worked on the truck, earning enough money to pay for college.

However, I would see them only if they were running late or I was early, and neither was the case that night. The dock at the Fairmont looked clean, and I could see the empty barrels stacked neatly in front of the freight elevator door; Jake and Rog obviously had been there and were gone already. Too bad, I thought—a little company and chitchat broke up the night, something I looked forward to. And this location wasn't the friendliest, another reason it was nice to have your friends in sight.

It was common to see derelicts here, down and outs who wandered the streets and called the alleys their home. They rarely bothered us garbagemen and we didn't bother them. Most were just looking for a place to sleep or a source of food, and wanted to be left alone. *Live and let live,* I figured. However, certain stories did circulate among the garbios, and I was told to watch out for the occasional loony on drugs.

As I backed in, the roar of the diesel engine and the glare of the work lights bolted to the top of my truck informed all the rats in the area I was coming, and that it was time for them to leave. I hoped they got the message. I applied the brakes and the sudden rush of air flowing from the tanks to the lines made the usual loud snap. I shifted the power takeoff into gear, flipped on the solenoid, jumped down from the cab, worked my way in the dark recess between the truck and the side dock, and climbed the crumbling old concrete stairway to the landing.

Sure enough, I thought, casing the place quickly, fifteen fiber drums of office trash, five barrels of restaurant garbage, one on its side, looked to be half-empty with its contents spilled, some cardboard stacked up neatly and more lying scattered about … and then I saw him—a big black man lying in the corner of the dock, with a doubled up sheet of cardboard for his bed. That was unusual, I thought. Ninety-nine percent of the time the bums would hightail it out of the area as soon as we showed our presence. The fact that he elected to stay put did not bode well.

He wasn't sleeping, just lying there with his eyes open and a strange look on his face. He didn't have the usual demeanor of fear, fatigue, poverty or long-suffering that most of his fellows had. This guy looked new to the streets, strong, his clothes not yet torn and dirty. And he was holding a knife. Now I didn't consider myself racist. The fact that he was black meant no more to me than if he was orange. But that look in his eyes and that knife in his hands were the two things that set him apart.

If I had a partner, I reassured myself, we would tell him to scram. At the least, we would have kicked him off the cardboard and cleaned up the mess. However, I didn't have a partner, and this guy did not seem in the mood to be moved. My job was to empty the dock of all rubbish. Not tonight, I figured. The cardboard he was lying on could remain.

He didn't look at me; he didn't even acknowledge my presence. He just stared straight ahead. His demeanor seemed to say, "Don't bug me, man. Just stay away."

I didn't say a word to my new found alley partner, but proceeded to empty one barrel and the next, and so on until they were all done. A sense of unease crept into my mind every time I turned my back. My imagination started to work.

I pictured him jumping up and driving the knife into my back, stealing my wallet, leaving me to die right there on the dock. I thought I could hear footsteps behind me every time I rolled a barrel to the truck, and my fear turned to anger. I pictured myself fighting him off and tossing him into the truck's hopper as I ran the compacting blade over his body. By the time I had run several loads into the truck, I was hitting the handle with enough force to almost break the connection. My feelings of fear were fighting with my sense of survival.

Yet, every time I turned to face what for sure I thought would be this charging lunatic with a knife aimed at my heart, there he was, still lying on his cardboard bed, unmoved. He must be biding his time, I thought to myself, slyly waiting for the opportune moment. Yet even as the loading dock became progressively emptier, my imagined attacker did nothing.

My fears subsided and I grew more rational. I realized he just wanted to be left alone. The thought that he would attack me was ridiculous, I reasoned.

By now, I had emptied all the barrels with the exception of the overturned container closest near him. As I moved to pick up that up, I noticed garbage lay scattered about the area that made his bed. The mess that he lay in must have come from the half-empty barrel that I was just now rolling away. I didn't quite understand the reason, yet it was obvious something had happened that night that didn't sit right with him.

The scattered sheets of flattened boxes were the last to go. I gathered the cardboard that lay near him, still not saying anything. The piece that he lay on would stay there for the night, I thought to myself. It'll be part of tomorrow's trash.

The dock was now empty except for the transient and his cardboard cot. Still no eye contact passed between the two of us, but I could sense an understanding had developed, nevertheless. I jumped down off the dock and left with a short "See ya." *Live and let live*, I figured. Climbing into my truck, I roared off into the night on to my next rendezvous with the city's trash.

* * *

That weekend, I met some of the guys at the neighborhood theater for a movie that had just opened. Rog Ouwinga was there. Part of the night's conversation led to our summer work on the truck. Rog chuckled a bit and asked if I had noticed anything different Wednesday night.

"No, not that I remember," I replied. "What are you talking about?"

He went on to explain how he had tipped over a barrel of garbage on this down and outer a few nights ago. He had noticed him sleeping, and while Jake was bringing the empties back up the freight elevator, he sneaked up to the dock, pushed the barrel over on the guy, and ran away.

"That'll show the lousy bums," Rog laughed, "to use the docks as their apartments. Man, they always make a mess, don't they, and then we get the blame."

He chuckled heartily, and thought that a funny thing to do. I laughed—kind of—and then informed him that the victim of his lighthearted prank was still there fifteen minutes later, with a knife in hand. I told Rog that I wished that he had been there to see the look on the guy's face, and, if necessary, to protect my back. For some strange reason, the humor of the situation escaped me that night.

7

The Big Hurt

July 1969

It was 3:10 on a Wednesday morning and I was guiding my Vander Puy & Son Disposal truck east on Roosevelt Road, heading into the city. The streets at this absurd hour were abandoned, with only an occasional car or truck breaking the stillness of the night. I never quite knew whether to be amazed at how empty the streets could be at this time or surprised that they weren't emptier.

My first three stops were in Lawndale, a West Side neighborhood of Chicago given over to derelict buildings and litter-strewn streets. What I was going for was a combination of only two dumpsters and eight drums of office paper. *Little shit*, I thought. I liked the big stops, the warehouses where I could pile yard upon yard of rubbish in the truck. I got loaded more quickly, and the larger stops usually meant larger entrances and less maneuvering of the truck. They were usually places with lots of lights, easy access docks, and people there to talk with. The little stops in remote, dark alleys didn't seem worth my while.

The fourth stop was to be an all-night greasy spoon on Western Avenue, about 2300 South. I had been here only once before and I followed my route book closely. One of the problems with filling in for summer, I realized, was being yanked from route to route, one truck to another, never really getting the hang of my duties. I would just be comfortable with one route and how it operated, when I would have to switch to a different one. Occasionally I would miss a stop; then realizing my error, I would have to go back, losing time doing so. The best way to get to the destination was not always clear. Often the street I chose didn't go through, ending at a train track, expressway, or major industrial plant. Of course, just finding the address wasn't enough. Sometimes it took a while to locate where they hid the garbage.

There was no way I could work as efficiently as the regular route-man, and that bothered me. I would try to make up for it by working as quickly as I could, rarely stopping to chat with any others I might meet.

To make matters worse, for the first time since last summer I was on a truck with the Leach packing system. In the previous weeks, I had gotten comfortable with a Heil packer and all its strangeness. For weeks, I had been pushing buttons and swinging bars, now I was pulling handles and grabbing at cables. *Oh well,* I thought, *I shouldn't complain. It's a job.*

A good paying job too, I was proud to say. I knew that some of my college friends who lived on the South Side made good money in construction, but from what I'd heard of others trying to earn tuition who lived in Wisconsin, Iowa or Michigan … it was a struggle. The guys were blown away when I explained how much I could make on the truck in a summer. I would regale them with stories of transients, rats, scary parts of the city, and the goodies I often found. *If this job was as good as I bragged to others,* I reminded myself, *I should keep this in mind the next time the alarm goes off at 2 AM.*

Working my way down Western Avenue, I scanned the addresses and street signs, struggling to determine where the restaurant was that Roger Groenboom and I picked up last week. Seeing some familiar territory, I realized I was getting close. The aging, dimly lit sign appeared in the next block and I felt a sense of relief. Finding the stop was often half the battle.

I pulled into the alley behind the café and stopped by the Dempster Dumpster. Going back to the business end of the truck, I realized that my vehicle was positioned on a slight incline, with the back end up. That shouldn't make a difference, I figured. I would attach the container to the packing blade with the cables, and the blade would 'cycle up' and draw the heavy steel box up against the back plates. The two ends of the box that were essentially round steel bars—I think the veteran garbios called them the elephant ears—should fit right in place. *If they didn't slide in,* I told myself, *I'd have to go move the truck … or do something.*

Pulling and pushing the heavy container filled with restaurant garbage, I maneuvered it into position as best I could. With the Leach system, those steel bars or 'elephant ears' had to slide in against a retaining wall for it to work correctly. If they slipped into the groove, the hydraulic power of the truck, using either chains or cables, would pull the box forward. If done right, the Dumpster would ride right up toward and into the hopper.

That was how it was supposed to work. I pulled the handle up and out, and the engine roared its assent. The packing cycle began and the box began to rise off the ground. However, because of the tilt of the truck in this alley, one end was not going in the groove. Rather quickly, I realized that if I didn't stop the process, the container would continue to go up at a bad angle and the entire box, all 1000 pounds or more, might fall into the hopper. I wasn't going to let that happen.

I quickly grabbed the handle; the howl of the engine ceased and probably some people trying to sleep in the neighborhood rolled over and smiled. The box remained slightly askew and not seated properly. I now realized that I had to relax the cable tension and start all over by rerunning the cycle, taking another fifty seconds. My impetuosity kicked in. There was another possibility. Perhaps I could save time if, by using brute force, I could grab the misaligned steel bar and push it where it didn't want to go.

Not smart!

At the precise moment I applied the necessary nudge, it literally flew the next two inches up against the wall of the truck's hopper, bringing my left hand with it. Two fingers were at the exact point of impact where the bar met the plate. In the nanosecond it took the sense of pain to reach my brain, my reaction was to yank my hand free. The next moment it was up and in the air. I knew damage had been done and I shook my hand out of shear desperation. Wetness spattered against my face in the dark. In a natural curiosity that my brain wanted to satisfy, I moved over to the lone light on a utility pole in the alley and held up my hand for a better view.

The two middle fingers had all flesh torn off for a full inch, leaving only bone protruding. I turned to look with astonishment at the point of impact where the half ton dumpster box had met the truck. There, caught in a vise between the two points of steel, remained my glove, frozen in position, with the fleshy remains apparently still inside.

By now, the full impact of what happened was beginning to register. Part of my brain told me I needed help before going any further. The other half pointed out

that the garbage had to be picked up and the truck cared for. I went to the cab door, managed to open it with my good hand, and reached up to turn off the engine. I could do no more. I left the truck parked with the box still attached and my work glove sticking out, presenting a stark image for any who would come upon the scene.

Now what was I to do, I asked myself? Here it was in the dead of night and I am in an alley behind Western Avenue, miles from where I knew anybody or anything. And I'm a cripple and in severe pain. I made for the front door of the café. Finding it open for business at this early hour, I decided at least something was working in my favor.

I opened the door and was bathed in an ugly fluorescent light. One man sat hunched over at the counter while the sole worker was wiping the countertop clean. I approached the man with the wash rag and stammered, "Hi—I'm from Vander Puy Disposal, picking up your garbage. I just had an accident. You got some bandages?" and held up my hand, to show the need.

Seeing the blood splattered across my face and my de-fleshed fingertips, the counterman, with a look of shock, replied, "Buddy, you need more than a bandage."

"Oh, damn, guy, whad' you do?" interjected the customer, now upright and fully awake.

"I just got my hand stuck in the truck." I said, in a somewhat apologetic manner.

"You gotta get to a hospital for that." The counterman pointed out. He thought for a minute. "Jack, can you take him or should I?" The other man was apparently a regular customer. But Jack didn't want to get involved or didn't like blood, "Hell no, you go ahead. I'll mind the store. St. Anthony's the closest. You be the Good Samaritan."

A moment later, I was in the stranger's car, holding my throbbing hand and headed for a hospital, three miles distant. Along the way, although my injury hurt mightily, I determined to act as if the pain had no effect on me. I was a blue-collar worker now, with gloves and boots, doing a man's job. Upon arrival I sauntered up, trying to be calm as a cucumber, to the front desk. Within minutes I was whisked to the emergency room, and the restaurant worker, my Good Samaritan, left, never hearing what became of the young man with the smashed fingers. I never knew his name.

By now, the pain in my hand had reached a plateau and, though still great, I had my emotions under control. I felt I was in good hands now, and there was obviously nothing life-threatening. I figured I could cope with this hospital stuff. I might be in pain, I told myself, but I can walk in under my own power. I wasn't going to show any weakness. I was twenty-one years old and at the top of my strength. This was simply a wound of war, so to speak, my own 'badge of courage,' as I recalled a book I had read last semester for Lit. 102.

A nurse motioned for me lie down and asked me how I was feeling.

"Fine." was the casual reply. She strapped me to the bed with a belt. I inwardly questioned the belt thing.

"Good," she coldly responded. "Cause this may hurt a little." She picked up my bloodied hand and, looking me in the eye, said "Relax your hand," and lowered it in a bowl filled with some liquid.

I've been told that all that came out of my lips was a howl, followed by silence. I have to take other people's words for it. I don't recall myself...I blacked out. So much for being Mr. Stoic.

8

Last Dreams

1969

This much we do know: due to the lack of identification papers on the corpse and the tattered clothes, the man was one of the homeless of the city, a transient without a place to call his own. Also, according to the autopsy, he was in his mid-forties, and his health was in a sorry state. Botulism was diagnosed in his system and the poor individual must have been experiencing bouts of pain on a regular basis.

Frank Boersma, mechanic for Leddenga Disposal, states that he had left open the door to truck number 23, and believes that the victim must have sneaked in that night. Stan Nydam, the other mechanic and the one who made the grisly discovery, swears that the door, as best he can recall, was closed when he went to start the truck, and that if it had been open he would have noticed. Stan, days later, mentioned to those close to him that he had had a dream that night that foretold what was to happen, but that it came back to him only after the fact.

It is also a well-known fact that graphic photos of the man's torso and his head were copied and pinned to walls of various disposal companies as warnings to all the employees.

What is not known, and probably never will be: what possessed the man to go up into the truck? This surely was not a comfortable place to be in. How long was he there? Why wasn't he able to get out in time?

Those at Leddenga Disposal as well as the police have speculated on answers for these mysteries. But they can only speculate …

* * *

Those pursuing were almost upon him when the transient saw the opening in the side of the truck. Some type of access door had been left open—here was an escape route seemingly just for him. There was no other out; it was this, or they would find him for sure. In desperation, he clambered up into the warm, shadowy truck body and quickly, yet quietly closed the door. Within seconds, he heard footsteps run past, the drunken teenagers swearing, laughing, and openly declaring what they would do to any 'damn bum' whom they could catch.

The vagrant, feeling very much like prey, laid still, his heart pounding, his lungs taking in great gasps of air, recuperating from his exertions. The sound of the hunters grew faint. In time, his breaths grew shorter, as he focused on the safety cocoon in which he found himself. He breathed a deep sigh and began to relax. He was just minding his own business, he reasoned. Why did those teenagers pick on him like they did? He wasn't bothering anybody. Why did they push him to the ground, kick him, and say those things about him? Being on the street, scrounging for food, money, and some sense of territory was hard enough. Now these punks were giving him a rough time.

He had been hanging out on the near north side of Chicago for a couple of years now, sleeping in hallways, living on the lower level of Wacker Drive, panhandling on the streets of the Magnificent Mile. The man couldn't recall what life was like living in a home, with people who cared, a regular time and place eat, sleeping in the same bed every night. He recalled he had that once, but it was a dim memory now. Now he eked out his life on a daily basis, just trying to survive. Food—shelter—clothes on his back. The bare bones of life. That was all he hoped for now; that was all he desired. That, and to be left alone in his misery.

A car drove by slowly, avoiding the gaping potholes in the road, and disappeared in the evening's shadows. He listened intently for the sounds of the night in the city. The distant steady pulse of the cars and trucks on the Kennedy Expressway, mixed with the locomotives pulling in and out of Union Station, formed a backdrop of the comforting, recognizable noises of his environment. Voices were another matter. Close voices were especially to be feared. Cars, trucks, and trains didn't hurt him; men could, and often did. The familiar sounds played upon his ears, and all else was quiet.

He relaxed. Now that he considered himself safe inside this truck, he hoped he could get a good night's rest. He told himself that he would lay low, right here. He'd wake early and sneak out before any security guards or police came around. He lay down and began to dream.

* * *

For the moment, this dweller of the downtown streets slept safe, although fitfully. The hours when he could sleep were the best of his day. His waking hours were consumed with walking the city's streets, begging from good people, and staying away from those who would do him harm. The nice ones would give him some pocket change or even a buck on occasion. The cops wouldn't give him too much grief, as long as he kept his distance from folks. Security guards were a little meaner, quicker to kick, throw, and swing. Occasionally the 'Man' would haul him off to jail for the night, or worse, to Cook County Hospital. There they would do all kind of things—strap him to a bed, stick needles in him, bathe him in cold, bright light, stare at him, talk about him, and then finally let him go. It was embarrassing to be brought to County. He did all he could to avoid it.

But his real concern was teenaged punks, the young bucks from the suburbs. They could be mean to transients like him. He heard stories of some like him being run over on purpose by kids in their cars, others set on fire, a few tossed in the river for fun. If he encountered the young ones, he retreated to the other side of the street, or disappeared down an alley or to Lower Wacker. That was his haven now—the alleys, the loading docks, or the lower level—his safe zones, where others hesitated to go.

His features were like any other transient on the streets of any city. Whether people called him a derelict, a vagrant, a bum, a hobo, or simply the homeless, he was lumped with all the others like him. They avoided him, for in many of their eyes he was a human animal, making others uncomfortable in their presence. His always-dirty appearance had become part of him. Being unable to wash, he carried a strong odor about him. His unkempt beard was matted with filth, and the castoff sport coat he bought for two dollars weeks ago had become stained in many spots. He was scraggly thin, a shadow of what he had once been, a lifetime ago. His thin, dirty gray hair flowed out from under an old cast-off baseball cap. He didn't fully understand the extent others were put off by him, but he knew that touching anybody was a definite no-no, and would get the police after him very quickly.

Sticking his MacDonald's coffee cup out for loose change had been difficult to do at first. By now he had grown comfortable with it and had begun to be more forceful in his pleadings. He didn't want to remain invisible to society. He wanted them to see him, to show concern for him, to have pity and to care. At one time he had pride, but hunger drove that away months ago. Now he was a sorry sight indeed. Those who came upon him kept a good distance to prevent touching his clothes or breathing the air he breathed.

Earlier today, the man's stomach had been hurting badly. His stomach was always hurting lately, he noticed. He needed food to calm it down. If he could snag a buck or two from the street and get a hamburger, that would take care of some of the pain. So he headed for Michigan Avenue to hit on people, knowing that if the right individuals came by, he might get some help, yet fearful, always watching for any who might do him harm.

* * *

By the time the second bell had rung, officially dismissing school, Ken VanKooten and Pete Bulthuis were already in the parking lot with Gary Hoving, Dan VanDyk, and Marty Mulder a hundred yards behind in hot pursuit. They were cracking up over the fact that old man Winfield hadn't noticed them sneak out the back. "This is how all weekends should begin, guys," Ken said, as the five gathered in the far corner, by two of their cars. "Out three minutes early, fun already starting."

The five seniors piled into Gary's 1961 Chevrolet and headed to the A & W to make plans for that evening. They argued amongst themselves about taking in a movie, heading downtown or following the dorks of the school to the track finals being held at Oak Lawn. However, when Gary produced the bottle of Southern Comfort from under his seat, the school function never had much chance. Watching a movie while being half drunk wasn't going to work either, they decided. Downtown Chicago it was to be.

* * *

It was the end of the working day at Leddenga Disposal. All the drivers had gone home; and Frank Boersma, the afternoon mechanic, was closing up the brick and concrete block garage on West Chicago Avenue. Finally close to 5:30 p.m., he was ready to head home. He followed his usual routine, doing last minute checks. The hydraulic fluids were filled, air tanks drained, and fuel tanks topped off. Stan Nydam, the morning mechanic, would take care of any slow leaks that would become a flat.

Frank had been busy today. He had fixed the broken packing blade on Unit 12; welding it with a brace to give it more strength to stand up to the punishment some of these asshole workers would put it to, he thought. He changed three flats this afternoon—about normal. The side mirror on truck #34 was re-attached, sturdier this time, so the driver wouldn't have it falling off in the middle of the Eisenhower, and, as he had vividly put it, 'couldn't see hide nor hair' for a few minutes as to what traffic was to his right.

That had to be scary—Frank knew. He was forty-seven years of age, and had been a mechanic for many years. Yet he remembered what it was like to drive these trucks in the streets and alleys of the city. He became a helper on an open truck for a few years right out of high school, back in the fifties, then moved up to driver for ten years or so. He could still recall the awe the workers had when the boss came in with the first packer garbage truck. However, the newer, better trucks didn't necessarily mean less work, just hauling more garbage in the day.

When his back started to go after putting in twenty-one years in the alleys, he asked for and got the mechanic's job. The pay was just as good and a lot easier on the body. Didn't have to go out in the heat and cold as those poor young suckers did, he thought.

He looked at his checklist and made a few notations. The clutch was going out on #15, Frank had been informed. He wasn't surprised. The young driver assigned to that truck couldn't get the hang of shifting with no clutch, and was wearing it out too fast. Frank would order the parts tomorrow, and either he or

Stan would put it in next week. And if the clutch goes sooner, Frank thought to himself, the young fool would have to use old # 7.

All the trucks were in the garage now but for the two parked outside, #35, with the broken hydraulic hose, and #23, with the messed up power take-off. That PTO had been acting funny lately, he admitted. Put it in gear one minute and it didn't work. Put it in gear the next and it worked fine. Go figure. Now it was in the mood for not working. Front blade all the way forward and not going back, no matter what he did. Body won't rise; blade won't cycle.

Frank left a note and his opinion on the matter for Stan Nydam to check out tomorrow first thing. Can't have another truck sit idle, Frank reasoned to himself. Have to keep them on the road where they make money.

* * *

A few blocks distant, the transient stumbled along to Michigan and Chicago Avenues, where he usually had good luck. Two weeks ago some girls had seen him, felt pity like they do sometime, gave him a couple bucks and some leftovers from Gino's. Last week three couples shared their leftovers from the ChopHouse and some change. A man could live quite well in this neighborhood, the derelict knew, as long as he was just left alone to do his thing.

His stomach was aching badly now and he didn't know what to make of it. The fact that he was suffering from botulism and that, in time, without medication, he would pass out, was lost on the poor soul. If he were lucky, he'd fall down on the street where the public would see him. Somebody perhaps would call the authorities, and they would put him in the hospital and he would survive. If he weren't lucky, he would collapse in a corner on Lower Wacker and die slowly and alone.

Stomach pains aside, he became aware that he had problems of greater concern right now. He observed them from a half block away, sauntering down Michigan. Five of what appeared to be high school kids were in the city this night, apparently already a little drunk and feeling bold. Seeing the transient in his dirty sweatshirt, floppy old gym shoes, and stained pants, was a clear signal for them—here was a victim waiting for their bullying. The 'group prod' took effect and the verbal abuse began instantly. Some hooting and hollering, a swiping of his coin cup, two or three violent shoves and the man figured his best chance was to get across the street and clear out. The young men followed a while, continuing to hound him; however, they tired of the game, stopped, and turned back.

* * *

Pete had been the first to suggest roughing the vagrant up—Pete's old man had a small business on north Clark Street and had had problems with the local bums for months. They were always getting into the dock area, messing with the trash, his dad complained. Ken agreed. From what he had heard from his cousin who worked for the Power Company, if anything in the storage yard wasn't nailed down, it would soon disappear, probably sold for scrap metal to get cash for alcohol or drugs. According to his cousin, all of the hobos of the city should be rounded up and put in jail.

The fifth of whiskey had been replaced by two six packs of Old Style and the boys were well on their way to becoming intoxicated when they saw the homeless man, begging on the corner of Michigan and Huron. When Pete knocked the cup out of his hand and the little amount of change scattered about on the sidewalk, the others laughed. The man swore back at them and tried to spit, but not much came out. If it hadn't been for the crowds of people on the sidewalks, an altercation might have started right then. The little act of self-defense got Gary angrier than the others, perhaps because the spittle landed closest to his shoe. He threatened to get physical with the next bum he saw. Marty suggested that they calm down, and recommended that they check out a pizza restaurant on Rush Street he had heard about. Muttering under their breath and acting tough, Gary and Pete feigned resistance, swore that they were ready to rid the town of all such low life. The others took this for the bravado it was, and pulled them along on their way to the food.

* * *

Frank Boersma made his final rounds. All doors were secured, the two dogs put in for the night, the truck windows washed, tanks filled with diesel ready for the next day. Only half the guys would be in tomorrow, it being Saturday. Stan Nydam, the other mechanic, would open things up at 5 a.m. Frank would be down by 10 a.m. Saturday was maintenance time, when the trucks were in most all day.

Before he left, Frank figured he would do Stan a favor. If he had to tinker with the inside of #23, the one with the bad POWER TAKEOFF, the smell would be overpowering in there. Frank decided he would open the access door to the main body of the truck where the garbage was compressed. This would air it out, he knew. Stan had done him a few favors, Frank recalled. He owed him one.

Reaching up and releasing the gate, he thought he heard some angry shouting a block away. Not unusual here, he knew, close to the action streets of Rush, Superior, and Ontario. Liquor and young bucks didn't mix, Frank reasoned, or rather, they mixed too well. That kind of city life was over for him however. He was ready to head home, to his wife and kids. As he got in his car and pulled out of the gravel lot next to the building, sirens were sounding, taxis honking, and the North Side of Chicago was coming alive.

* * *

Two hours and numerous beers later, as they negotiated the unfamiliar streets of uptown Chicago, the five teenagers were feeling the effects. Cutting in front of cabs on Michigan and almost being hit in the process only added to the excitement. After the pizza place owner realized they had sneaked out without paying, he ran after them a ways before giving up. They pictured themselves really 'bad dudes' now and figured they might as well play the part to the full. They would act out their fantasies of being big time big-city hoods. That scraggly old bum who dared to disrespect them a while ago, any other teens that they might meet downtown tonight, perhaps even some office windows—all would be fine recipients of their targeted rage against authority.

The derelict in question worked his way up and down the streets of Michigan, Rush, and Dearborn. Getting close to 10 p.m., yet still there were a few productive hours for him to stay on the street. He had gotten his share of dirty looks, handouts of food, seven or more dollars, and some religious tracts. This was an average night, except for that run-in with those five young ruffians. His stomach wasn't throbbing now. The cheap drink he was working on dulled the pain. He figured that by midnight he would have enough food stashed in his hiding place on Lower Michigan Avenue. Hell—with a few more bucks he told himself, he could even pay for a shower at the YMCA.

As the man crossed Huron Street, he heard someone shouting, noting that some swearing was directed at him. He turned and saw on the other side of the street the same five guys who had given him a rough time earlier that evening. He knew he had to think quickly. He headed for the nearest alley but before he could get there to disappear in the shadows, they were up to him, and the pushing and mocking began. There wasn't much for him to do, but to take it and hope they would tire of this bullying soon. One of them grabbed him by his coat and threw him to the pavement. He protected his body as best he could, falling to the ground and curling into a ball. After several well-placed kicks that drew gasps of deep pain, the youths tired of their antics and began to discuss what to do next. They became distracted and argued amongst each other. The man struggled to his feet and slowly, discreetly moved away. If he could just disappear into the recesses of his city, he would be fine, he thought.

With their attention diverted, he got a half block away when two of them took note and decided a chase would be fun. That is when he made his mistake. He took flight and ran. Scared now, he swore to himself, as he knew he erred in fleeing. Yet, he ran with surprising speed for his age of forty-two years. He knew the dead ends, the stairs, the loading docks, the trash containers, and inner walkways in which to hide. This kept him out of their reach for while, and gave him hope that he would yet be able to escape their torment. He knew he wouldn't be able to outrun them in a foot race.

Using all the street smarts he knew, he eluded them in a strange kind of foxhunt, he being the prey, and the young men, thinking this the highlight of the night, on his tail. Just as the hunter adrenaline rises in the chase, so also did the teens in their pursuit of the poor man. As the manhunt moved from the well-traveled streets of the near North Side to the more degraded industrial area, the transient realized there was a greater chance of some major hurting coming his way if they caught him. He had to find a place to hide permanently, and stop trying to outrun these kids.

Staying in the shadows as best he could, he found himself near the Leddenga Disposal garage and truck lot. He knew this area well; he conjectured that this territory might be his sanctuary. As he slipped into the fenced area where he knew a hole in the barbed wire to be, he could hear the dogs inside the garage barking. He also sensed that the young men were only a hundred yards down the street and coming fast. Then he spotted an open steel door in the side of one truck. In desperation he pulled himself up into the warm, dark body and quickly closed the metal door. Within seconds, he heard footsteps run past, the teenagers swearing, laughing, and declaring what they would do to any damn bum they could catch.

He laid still, his heart pounding, his lungs taking in great gasps of air, recuperating from his exertions. The sound of the hunters grew faint. In time, his breaths grew shorter, as he focused on the safety cocoon in which he found himself. He breathed a deep sigh and began to relax. The sound of the hunters continued to become faint and he began to examine his surroundings. He had never done this before. He thought he knew all the hiding places of the city, and was pleased he had found a new one. This haven was warm and dry. The odor was strong and pervasive, but it was safe. This may have some prospect for the future, he thought.

Now that he was secure inside this truck, maybe he could get a good night's rest. That is what he would do, he thought to himself … crash right here. He'd wake up early before the workers came and sneak out. He lay down and in a few minutes was sound asleep, dreaming of his life of long ago, when he was young, when he was happy.

* * *

Stan Nydam's clock went off at the usual time, 4 AM. In the pre-dawn darkness, he reached out and, in the usual swipe, pushed off the irritating sound for another several minutes of snoozing. In a moment, he was back asleep, dreaming. He was working on a truck's hydraulic system, but for some reason the vehicle, while he was examining the hoses, began to drive under its own control. He continued to work while the vehicle meandered down the streets of the city. Now the truck became a box with open ends at either side, and he was at one end. Stan saw a stranger in this truck-become-box. For some reason, he began to slowly close one end. He heard the man cry out as if to say Stop, but no words came out of his mouth. The stranger had a horrified look on his face, and as he was wondering why, Stan awoke with a start when the alarm sounded for a second time.

He stumbled out of bed and cursed mornings like this. Wrested from a deep dream and rudely brought into reality, he forgot what he was seeing so vividly a minute ago. He went through his morning rituals, ate a breakfast of toast and eggs, grabbed his second cup of coffee for the drive in to the city, and went out the kitchen door into the early morning light.

Leaving his house at 4:40, Stan scheduled this ride in from the North Side so he would arrive at the Chicago Avenue garage by 5 AM. The city seemed beautiful this morning, he thought. The sun was just rising and casting sheen on the mountains of limestone, steel, and brick. The Hancock, the Drake, and all the high-rise buildings along Lake Shore Drive were in a fiery glow of orange and white. Combined with the blue-gray of Lake Michigan to the east, the scene that seemed to be for his eyes alone gave brilliance worthy for a postcard photograph. He wondered if any camera people ever got up at this time of the day and saw this sight.

Stan pulled in the parking lot on West Chicago, locked his car, and opened the doors to the garage. The dogs greeted him with anticipation, scampering in circles, eager for the coming food and water. They had come to know that when this human being arrived, soon others would come as well and their long, lonely night was over.

* * *

The transient half awoke from some noise that he could not clearly identify, took note of where he was, still safe inside his truck shelter. No sound of the teenagers any more. He didn't know what time it was, but they had to be gone by now. He closed his eyes again and figured he could sleep another hour before he had to worry about being seen by anybody. In a moment, he was back in his dream world of long ago friends and family.

A few hundred feet away Stan checked Frank's notes of the afternoon before, and then examined the trucks' tires. "Glory be, no flats today," he exclaimed to the dogs, who showed their joy by barking. He opened the big overhead doors in preparation for starting the engines, raised the hoods, checked the oils, and after filling a few, fired them up. By now, some of the drivers were arriving, ready to pull out at 5:30.

Everything on Frank's checklist was done except for the PTO or power takeoff problem on #23, the one with a sticky switch. "For some crazy reason," Frank had written, "sometimes it helps to have the PTO in gear before starting it up. It don't make sense," the note went, "but it works. Go figure!"

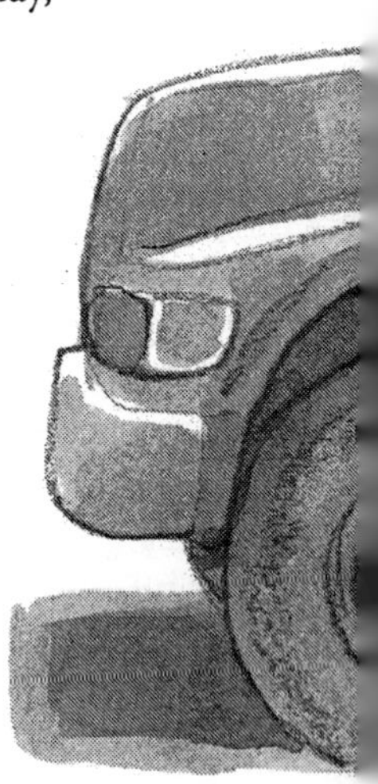

Stan went out to the truck yard and, climbing in, engaged the power takeoff before pushing the starter button. He turned the key; the gauges did their thing, all indications that everything was normal. Let's try it, he thought to himself. He pushed the button and the Cummins 240 rumbled to life.

* * *

The transient had become dimly aware of the presence of someone outside the truck, yet in his dream, he was in bed at his folk's place and still in grade school. That was simply his dad outside in the driveway, getting ready to leave for work.

Reality jolted him awake. As the thunderous roar of the diesel engine reverberated in the steel box surrounding him, the man noticed, now that the light of dawn was trying to penetrate the inside, a wall on one end of his shelter was moving toward him. In a moment, he understood the situation he was in. This steel partition was coming closer and closer until it would crush him against the other side.

Exerting every effort to move as fast as he could to the access door, he tried to leap over the four-inch thick piston drawing the wall to him and slipped on the shiny, well-oiled steel surface. Instantly, his left foot became trapped under the pulsating piston and a stab of pain shot through him as the steel pin ground against his ankle.

In sheer terror now, as he realized what would happen within seconds, he yanked his foot free, tearing his shoe off in the process. He dove for the door,

pushed it open, and got his head out, even as the wall approached. Any further movement was stopped by his shoulders as the moving partition came upon him. The five hundred pound blade of hardened steel methodically continued in its direction and pushed his body back even as his face was protruding out the door. In one second, he lost consciousness and in three, his head was detached from the body. The blade of the compacting mechanism, meant to push garbage out, continued its interminable journey to meet the retaining barrier of the closed tailgate, where it automatically stopped, but not before crushing the decapitated body inside. The other part lay on the ground next to the truck, a full ten feet away.

* * *

It was 10 a.m. and Stan Nydam, still visibly shaken but starting to calm down a little, related the story for the fourth time. John Leddenga had come down immediately when he got the call, and was doing what he could to assure his mechanic that it wasn't his fault. The cops duly took their notes and official photos. Even the county coroner's office was involved in this one. The word had spread, and now the media descended upon the Chicago Avenue garage to get the gruesome details.

It was a foolish, foolish thing to do, someone observed. Both the drivers and the police speculated as to why the man had chosen to climb into the body of the truck. In time the story of how the homeless wretch died, accompanied by a few grisly pictures, spread from driver to driver, company to company. Many a garage supervisor used it and the stark photos as a warning on taking safety precautions.

All who were at the scene felt compassion for the man and wondered what his last seconds were like. The two parts of the unfortunate were immediately put into a body bag. The blood on the gravel parking lot had been washed away as best the workers could, but one could still detect a red stain in the gravel. There remained a considerable amount in the back of the truck, but no one looked in there, for the access door was now closed.

* * *

About the same time that Saturday morning, many miles away, several young men were just crawling out of bed. They all had headaches, and recalled that they had been partying down in Chicago the night before. Yet none could remember exactly what areas of the town they visited or the places they had gone. They would get together Monday morning at school to rehash the weekend's events. Gary and Pete would recall something about a restaurant owner getting mad at them for some reason. Marty would remind them that they had had fun chasing a homeless man down some streets. However, this Saturday they had other, more pressing things on their minds. Dan had promised to go golfing with his dad, Gary headed off to sports camp, Ken and Pete reported to their part-time jobs, and Marty drove up to Fox Lake to fish.

9

Cook County Jailhouse Gray

1971

The radio crackled to life and a squawky voice filled the cab, "Base to fifteen, Base to fifteen."

Completing a shift as I crawled south on the Kennedy Expressway, I grabbed the mike off the dash, "Fifteen here, base. Go ahead."

"Fifteen, got a pick up at Cook County Jail on California Avenue, near 31st. Thirty-yard open box. Over."

"Roger" I replied. "I know where that is." The flow of traffic picked up and I shifted to a higher gear.

"Fifteen? You read me? The box is full of paint, barrels of paint, to be exact. Bring it to CID down south."

"Gotcha." I paused, thought a bit. "Are they OK with that?" A Yellow Cab quickly cut in front of me, and my open expanse of highway again narrowed to fifty feet. I hit the brakes and uttered something.

"Yea, they don't like it, but they know about it. In addition, Lar... boss says the barrels are old, falling apart. He's seen 'em. Says to be careful. We don't want a mess."

"Roger—out." Sounded like an easy stop, I thought to myself. I shouldn't have to tarp it. That meant I shouldn't get too dirty either. But there was a tone of warning in the dispatcher's voice, like he was a little worried, and I should be concerned. The cab now squirted over to the left lane and the entire flow was picking up. Well, it's just paint, I reminded myself. Let's check it out.

With a quick look in my mirrors, I moved to the right lane to exit on to the Eisenhower and headed for California Avenue. Since I had been driving the streets of Chicago that summer of 1971, I picked up the habit of talking to the bulldog ornamentation on the hood of my truck and whose visage also appeared on my steering wheel. "So, Mack, they want me to pick up a box loaded with rusting containers, filled with paint. Toss 'em, the guy tells me, at CID, that huge dump, er, landfill on the Southside."

I had signed on to work for a mid-size disposal company as temporary replacement for drivers on vacation. I was driving what some called a roll-off, others a box truck, designed for carrying portable containers ranging in size from fifteen to seventy cubic yards of anything from paper waste to crushed rock to overstocked candy from a warehouse.

Recently I had been teaching in the clean environs and rural landscape of southern Minnesota where 'pollution' was cow manure on the road, and farmers recycled nails from old barns before tearing them down.

However, I was a native of this asphalt jungle called Chicago and knew the way of thinking here. If it was slightly old, toss it. If it was no longer wanted, put it in a landfill and forget about it. If it had to be done, it had to be done. Full speed ahead and damn the environment.

"Well, this sounds like a fine example of bureaucratic inefficiency," I commented to my friend on the wheel, swinging through the Spaghetti Junction where the Dan Ryan, Kennedy and Eisenhower Expressways meet.

Heading west, I thought this through. Sounds like enough paint to cover every jail cell in the complex maybe twice over, and it all was to be discarded. Couldn't this be sold to a painting contractor? Wasn't there some church or school to which it could be donated?

Mack didn't have an opinion today, but I surely did. And to put all of this in the ground? The waste of the city had become all too obvious to me, and I was starting to be irritated by it.

I was twenty-three years old and not overly into the environment. Yet, even I could understand that just burying all that paint didn't seem a good idea. However, orders were orders, from the top on down. So, even if others in the chain of command had the same concerns, the paint had to be disposed of. I exited the Ike onto California.

By the time I got to the Cook County Jail Complex, it was 12:30 and my day was almost done. This would probably be the last trip, I was hoping. I pulled in the driveway and stopped at the security gate. I didn't have to get out of the cab; apparently, the dispatcher had made the calls and the guard motioned to me to proceed.

County Jail is a large place, I learned. As I navigated my way through the lanes and back lots, I spotted the red container with my company's emblem on it about two hundred yards off in the distance. Heading in that direction, I contemplated the very thin windows, the barbed wire fences, and the guard towers, all reminiscent of concentration camps I had seen in movies.

"I can just pick up this box and go my merry way out of here," I told Mack. "Here I am, sweating from the heat of the engine under my cab, dirty from the crap I have to deal with, and weary from getting up at 4 AM. But I'm free to drive right out of this place. It is good to occasionally put things in perspective, isn't it?"

Mack agreed.

As I pulled up to the open thirty-yard container, I could see eighteen drums inside, all in neat rows. Yep, they were showing their age. Two looked especially vulnerable to any rough treatment. I backed my rig to line up with the rails and cable hookup. Putting on the air brake, I climbed down to attach the cable to the heavy, inch-thick steel claw extending out from under the container.

After examining the 8 by 24-foot steel box, I made sure the gate was closed, safety chains attached and that nothing would fly out going down the road. A roll-off with a load like this doesn't come around every day, I thought. It's clean, no paper or anything to litter the highway. I won't have to tarp it; I just have to make sure I don't paint the roads on the way there.

Climbing back in and putting on the power takeoff, I engaged the clutch, raised the rpm's and slowly lifted the box onto the hoist, being as gentle as the hydraulic system would allow. Like Base said, the barrels were showing rust and would not take a lot of vibration. I could not have gray paint pouring out the back of my truck as I traveled the streets of Chicago. After pulling the cable tight so the box wouldn't slip and jostle, I lowered the hoist. Gently ... gently ... I thought to myself. The rails with their load of paint returned to the bed of the truck with a soft thud. So far—so good. I proceeded back out the way I came in.

I reported to the guard gate, convinced the officer I hadn't any escaping convict in my truck, got the ticket signed, and climbed back into the cab. As I pulled out onto California, I was already thinking about the nearby train crossing that I had to deal with before the highway. If I hit those tracks wrong, my truck would receive some bone-jarring jolts. I did not want to play paint mixer with my rig.

Approaching the crossing, I slowed to a crawl, yet still winced as the truck body reverberated over both sets of tracks. As I continued to navigate the streets of the near South Side, every bump and pothole jarred my load and my confidence. "How much more jostling can these damn drums take?" I asked Mack. "Can't the aldermen get the roads around here fixed?"

The bulldog did not want to get political today and remained silent.

Soon the expressway came in sight. "Finally," I said aloud. "The Ryan and a smoother ride. But .....also more cars and drivers to see if I am leaking." The expressway is a very public place on which to drive, I thought.

My two-way radio sputtered to life, the dispatcher at the base calling for my location. "Base to fifteen, what's your 10-20? Over."

"Just entering the Ryan, heading south." I responded.

"Roger." A pause. "Boss wants to know ... how's the load?"

"Got the barrels OK... they're holding... everything is fine." I lied.

"That's good, fifteen." I could detect a note of surprise and maybe a bit of non-belief. "Call in after you dump."

I entered the Dan Ryan at 47th Street, avoiding the rough spots as best I could, heading south. All the while I kept an eye on my mirrors, hoping I wouldn't see a wet gray line behind me. Or a cop car. 63rd Street ... 71st ... 75th ... The dump was at 130th, a ways to go. "Man," I complained to the bulldog. "This trip is taking forever."

About a mile before 95th, I thought I saw a squad car a ways behind me, coming up on my rear. Or, was that just a Chicago Transit Authority vehicle with those lights on top? A minute later, I could see for sure ... Shit, that is a cop and he is coming up fast. I was convinced he was after me for sure, probably sees paint pouring out and I'm getting a major ticket.

To my relief, he quickly passed on my left. Either I wasn't spilling, or he was on someone else's tail and didn't see, didn't care.

As the landfill drew closer, I began to relax. So far, so good, I thought. I might make it. I got off the Ryan at 111th Street and onto the frontage road. As I made the turn, I thought I could see a thin line of liquid going out the tailgate. Or was that just my imagination.

"Maybe some water on the bottom of the container," I said to Mack, talking aloud now to the hood ornament to ease my nerves. "Even if it is paint, this place isn't as busy as the Ryan. Fewer drivers to see it, mostly truckers. They ain't gonna care."

More silence from my buddy. I realized he wasn't going to give support. I continued regardless. "But now if a cop was to see me, and they do go up and down this road looking for this very thing ...."

About a mile ahead, I knew there was the set of 'train tracks from hell'. Two hundred yards before the entrance to the landfill, a railroad crossing, as old and in bad a shape as anywhere on the South Side, and a real rib shaker. It seemed to be a last ditch attempt by an unseen force to rattle loose what refuse it could to keep it from entering the landfill.

I approached the tracks cautiously. The gaps in the old wood railroad ties and cracked pavement seemed more ominous today. I slowed to less than ten mph, yet the quivering of the truck caused sickening sounds to come from the roll-off box. As I went through the gears, picking up speed again, I checked my mirrors for the umpteenth time. My little stream of liquid was growing. That's not water, I admitted to myself with an air of resignation. There was nothing I could do but continue. Only a half mile now to the dump and off the road.

I entered the landfill and proceeded on the winding driveway to the office. I worried. If I have to sit in line behind a string of trucks for any length of time dripping gray, I figured, some important people around here aren't going to like it. I rounded the final turn and could see the office area. Good, I thought, only two trucks in line.

I waited, concerned about who might pull in behind me and notice what my rig was doing. By this time, the truck, leaky container and all, had become an extension of me, and now a personal thing. I was doing a no-no and I knew it. I felt like I was urinating publicly and hoping no one would notice.

Minutes passed. Man, I groused, the drivers seem to be taking an eternity in the office. Probably yucking it up in there and I'm leaking out here. I glanced in my mirrors and saw two trucks coming in behind me. Well, go ahead and look, people. Pissing gray paint on the driveway.

Finally, the two drivers came out as a pair, all smiles. I was irked but tried to hide it. They pulled away and I inched forward, ready to get in and out as fast as I could. Rather than go directly to the office door, I had to satisfy my curiosity, and so I walked around the back of the truck.

I was spilling all right. There appeared a steady drip, drip, drip of strong smelling paint from under the tailgate. A small puddle had already formed on the concrete below. I glanced back along the road leading up to the office. I could see my trail of gray on the pavement. I'm standing still! I thought. What had it looked like moving down the highway? How much paint had I applied to the roads of the South Side of Chicago?

I scurried into the office, all smiles. Got the ticket OK. The man looked at me somewhat curiously, I thought. Or was I imagining this stuff? Again, like a moth to the flame, I took the long way behind the truck to my cab, so the image of paint dripping could sear into my brain. I passed in front of the next trucker in line. I forced a casual greeting to him and I could see the smile on his face as if he was laughing with me and the mess I was making.

Back in the cab and driving onto the pothole-ravaged gravel road to the dumping area, I could hear the barrels bouncing and rolling in the box. There was no help for it now. This was going to be one heck of a ride the rest of the way. By now, the gray out my back end had become a steady stream.

By the time I approached the final hill, in sight of the bulldozers and compactors, the 55-gallon barrels were dancing around like so many pinballs, and the stream of paint had turned into a river. I was leaving a trail of gray that extended a full half-mile or more. Yet soon I would be relieved of my tattle-tale box. Within minutes, I would be backing into the dumping zone and getting rid of the evidence. No cops had seen me on the road, and I felt I had dodged a bullet.

I maneuvered my truck as best I could so as the bulldozer operator couldn't see my tailgate area well and began to back up into the spot he was pointing to. Guiding my truck back a hundred feet to the soft zone, I braked and breathed a sigh of relief. Success!

By this point, I was dying to see what my load had become. I grabbed my gloves, clambered out of the cab, and sauntered back to the scene of the crime. Unhooking the safety chain, I swung open the gate, and saw that the entire floor and lower walls were coated in jailhouse gray. It puddled in the middle and had poured through a hole in the bottom of the roll-off box and onto my double wheels. My vehicle had turned into a rolling paintbrush. I climbed back in the cab, engaged the power takeoff, raised the body, and the drums and paint poured out. By now, the barrels were all trashed and I was essentially dumping empties. The paint I was to bring to the landfill had, instead, been spread out in an ever-widening trail for the past several miles.

I did some mental calculations. Eighteen barrels at fifty-five gallons per made for a little less than one thousand gallons of gray oil base paint. Many years previously, possibly before I was born, some bureaucrat had made a requisition, a clerk had signed the check, the taxpayers had footed the bill, and some painting contractor had intended to apply this finish to the floors and walls of the County Jail. For some crazy-ass reason it was never done.

Instead, the barrels had been allowed to sit for years and just rust away. Now it was decorating the roads leading up to the landfill. The lead, benzene, linseed oil, and other ingredients would percolate through the ground and along the surface of the roads for weeks, months, perhaps years to come. "But," as I explained to my ever-present counsel and friend, "there wasn't nothing I could do about it, Mack. I'm just doing my job." The face on my wheel just looked back at me and said nothing.

I picked up the microphone to report my position. "Unit fifteen to Base, fifteen to Base."

After a moment's pause, the tepid reply, "Base here."

"This is fifteen on the south side. I'm dumped and got an empty thirty-yarder on. Where to?"

A moment of silence on the other end and, if I could see along the radio waves, probably a relieved face.

"Hey, good job, garbio."

"What?" I asked.

"Never mind, Larry. Just drop that box at the government warehouse at Carroll Ave. and Sangamon St. Then come on home."

"Sounds good. 10—4"

"Larry, take note of where you place that container. You'll be picking it up tomorrow. They tell us they got 24,000 lb. of spoiled fruit."

"That's a 10—4, Base."

Like I told Mack ... just doing my job.

10

Garbio Gaffes

Laboring in the waste management industry is an inherently dangerous thing to do. That isn't news to the worker bees out on the streets and alleys of America. I've been there, done that and can attest to the fact that accidents often happen.

Hurrying was second nature to a garbageman when I worked on the truck. Handling already dented and dirty containers does not call for slow, deliberate treatment. Every worker knows that he is destroying what he is handling, and this mindset can develop a nasty habit of being hard on almost anything he lays his hands on.

Moreover, for many garbagemen, there is a finite amount of trash to pick up in one day. When that has been taken care of, his duty is done and he can go home. Seldom would one's boss give advice to work cautiously, double check one's calculations, redo that last block, and rearrange the last twenty cans emptied.

Consequently, many young men, especially those who like to be physical, love the job in spite of the brutal demand on the body. I have often speculated that a study of garbagemen might find that a high number have Attention Deficit Hyperactivity Disorder. The machinery they use promotes the mindset of 'hurry up and destroy.' The ponderous packing blades and push-out mechanisms are noisy and dangerous, and they obliterate objects wonderfully well. It is a few steps up from the little boy on a living room floor with his wooden hammer and blocks, just whaling away in delight.

So, if you can work fast and not be penalized for the speed; if you can demolish 98% of what you get your hands on and not pay for your actions; and if you wrap yourself with leather gloves and heavy duty, steel-toed boots, you develop an air of invincibility. Is there any wonder why a high number of accidents occur in the business?

* * *

Sometime in the 1980's

The crabapple and cherry trees of the Illinois spring were in full color, the blossom petals now falling lightly when an occasional tuft of wind drifted from the south. The walks and flowerbeds were fringed with fragrant little necklaces of pink and white, remnants of the landscaper's efforts to sweep the spacious lawn. Warm breezes brought out the smell of blossoms on the trees, and the lilacs, daffodils, and tulips were showing off their beauty.

Approaching the Holland Home for the Elderly, I walked along perfectly manicured turf, reflecting on when and if I would someday live here. Outside, amidst the re-birthing process, the temperature was 71°, just right for this mid-May afternoon. Inside, surrounded by the decaying process, the setting on all the thermostats was for a warmer envelope. I opened the top button of my shirt and removed my hat, out of deference to the temperature more than to the residents residing there.

I had come to visit with several of the elderly men. This spacious, modern senior citizen center was one of the larger and better run in the western suburbs. To it came many of the old men I had known in my younger years. The names on the doorways leading to each apartment and room read like a roll of a 1950s Calvinist church. Rozema, Van Zwieten, Tolsma, Bos, DenBoer, Vanden Bosch, Swierenga—the listing of surnames stemming from the flatlands of the Netherlands—trailed in to all the corridors and hallways.

Scattered amongst these Dutch-Americans were four men with whom I had made an appointment: Paul DeGraaf, Teunis Riemersma, Jake Ouwinga, and John Van Otten. These four had wrestled, in one way or another, with the trash and refuse of the city for much of their lives. And all four were widowers, having lost their wives from various illnesses. In the twilight of their years, these men enjoyed each other's company, as if they were again schoolboys on the streets of the old West Side.

DeGraaf I had probably known the longest, having been a neighbor for several years when I was a young boy. He always seemed to have a smile on his face. Although he was twenty-five years my senior, he had always been Paul and never Mr. DeGraaf. And it was he who first demonstrated to me the fascinating spectacle of the front cab of a container truck literally jumping up off the ground. To see a grown man sitting in his rig waving from ten feet above the street was indeed an impressive scene for a nine year old boy.

Riemersma and Ouwinga were simply two of the men in the close-knit community of which I was part. They had had families, although none of their children were near my age. Riemersma attended the same church as did my family, and my impression was that Ouwinga had been one of the pillars of the community, and an elder in the other house of worship, the one with the big white steeple. However, I did not really come to know them and appreciate their lives until I too had entered the territory of adulthood. I did know that both had duly served in church and school leadership positions and in my eyes, for that alone, they deserved respect.

Van Otten was the first to hire me on the garbage truck. He and his family operation struggled to make it against the growing behemoths in the industry. In time, his namesake business was absorbed, fading into history along with many others.

Among these four, I knew that their experiences and memories would soon be gone, and before that time came, I wanted to garner what information I could.

Scavengers enjoy recalling great calamities in the business. There are the classics, and over the years, I heard many of them. I had a hunch, however, that these garbios had tales I hadn't heard. I knew these old men had 'garbage in their blood.' I was also aware of their love to gab, to joke, and to spin the occasional stretcher. I reasoned that they would be excellent storytellers.

I met my friends in the lounge of the southwest quadrant called the Cicero lounge. They seemed lethargic at first, sitting around the television. I asked them to go outside with me, and the warmth in the air seemed to perk them up a bit. We sat with the sun bathing our faces for a while, not saying much, as we observed the landscaping crew cutting the lawn and tending the flowers. These elderly friends made some comments on the quality of the grass, the skills and speed of those running the mowers. The fresh smell of cut grass floated our way, and DeGraaf was the first to open up, commenting on the wondrous fragrance, so much a part of spring.

He was seventy-one years of age and had developed a pronounced limp that he said was a result of his forty years hauling garbage. He always kept his cane handy, and couldn't walk any distance without aid from an attendant. Paul DeGraaf talked in pure Chicago slang.

"Man, ain't dis new-cut grass smelling great, guys? Reminds me of playing the links, or da days when we played slow-pitch. I just luv it. I don't dink dere's anything better dan da smell of grass when it's been cut."

"You wouldn't be saying tat if you were out on te streets now picking up all the newly-cut grass." Riemersma interjected. "Trouble is, it ton't stay new very long. It has a tifferent odor to it after tays in the can, mixed wit rain and cookin' at ninety degrees, I'll tell ya. You city workers never had to smell tat stuff, did ya?" He finished with a well-aimed spit at the grass as if to indicate his displeasure for its sins of yesteryear.

Teunis Riemersma just turned sixty-nine, and though he had owned his own business in the city briefly, he worked most of his thirty-two years on residential garbage, running the streets, probably picking up his fair share of grass. He claimed that his healthy condition was precisely because of that daily regimen. While it was true that he seemed to be completely mobile in his walk, his eyesight was quite poor and he needed glasses to see with any sense of clarity. I discovered he rarely used them. I could detect a strong Old World accent that his fifty-eight years of living in America had not entirely removed. He had the annoying habit of often spitting after he talked, and I soon learned not to direct questions to him.

John Van Otten stepped in, "Riemersma, tell the truth. A lot of the grass was in bags. You didn't have it all that hard, picking up little bitsy bags." He was the youngest of the four, only sixty-five, and yet, in some ways, was showing signs of aging. He had recently picked up the unusual habit of wearing two watches on his left arm. When I asked him why he had two watches on his arm, he explained that he kept the one correct by synchronizing it with the other, although I discreetly noticed that neither was keeping correct time.

"Tat's true later, I'll admit. Folks stopped putting te grass in cans when bags became popular. Tey would break sometimes, too. Specially when I was going fast, whipping tem in two at a time. I remember a couple times, trowing a bag and it breaking in mid-air, grass flying all over te place. Wat a mess! Ten I wished tey still used cans."

Jake Ouwinga, the only one of the four to have never worked for anyone else, was the oldest at seventy-five years. Over the years he had built up one of the larger trash-hauling companies in Chicagoland, American Disposal, at one time employing almost two hundred drivers, mechanics and office staff. For upwards of three decades, his distinctively colored vehicles—a red, white, and blue mix—could be seen around the western regions of the city proper and suburbs. Along with that success, came the prerequisite societal demands. Appropriately, Ouwinga had been a leader in his church for years, and of the four, spoke with the most authority and was always poised.

Due to a stroke in his sixties, he was now consigned to a wheelchair. His eyesight was also somewhat impaired and he wore glasses with thick lenses. And, unlike his colleague Riemersma, Ouwinga used them. He chimed in, "Well, you men on house garbage often made messes." I noticed that Ouwinga often started his conversations with *well.* "I'd see the workers on my street, running—running—make a mess—stop—pick it up—then run some more. I always tell my men to slow down. That how accidents happen!"

I saw my opening and made the best of it. I asked the men about the messes, the calamities, and the great goofs that they could remember from their days in the business. I inquired of any legends and rumors that they had heard of from other garbagemen over the years. I knew of a few, I explained, and wanted to hear more.

"Why are you bringing up accidents, young man?" questioned Ouwinga. "Our business didn't have anymore than the others."

DeGraaf rolled his eyes and Riemersma answered, "*Ik dink dat het niet waar is.* Ouwinga, course we tid. Tink back, you old fool. You forgetting already?"

Van Otten rose to my defense as well. "You're right, son. The workers in the scavenger industry had a lot of mishaps. Some years more guys got hurt doing garbage than doing any other job."

He looked at me. "What do you want to hear?"

I first asked about the serious accidents that are part of garbage lore. Their withered faces showed pain when I mentioned those. I recalled the story I had heard years earlier of the juvenile game of "road chicken" that two truck drivers played a few blocks from the incinerator on Laramie Avenue. The story went that neither driver was able to straighten his vehicle in time, and all, drivers and crew, were killed. Was that true, I wanted to know?

DeGraaf verified it was, and then reminded us of the incident when a driver fell into the incinerator on the north side. "According to my brudder Jim, who heard it from da guy's wife, dey dink he musta been knocked out cold by da swinging tailgate, probably falling in wit da garbage. No one ever saw nuttin'. The man musta got suffocated or died from all dat weight of what landed on him."

"Ton't just tink tat it was just te guys on te truck tat could get hurt," Riemersma pointed out, "bad tings happened to oters too. Remember tat young VanderBroek boy? He was working under a packer truck, doing mechanic stuff, when anoter man—I know who it was too, but won't mention his name—hopped into te cab and not knowing te kid was under te truck, drove off, with the te rear doubles rolling right over him, killing him."

We paused for a while to digest that scene. Two robins fluttered to the ground not more than five feet from us, the one cocking its head and seeming to listen for food in the grass, its mate turning its eye on the five strange forms close by. The image of a human's sudden, brutal death in the way just described lay heavily on my mind. Riemersma spat again on the ground and, as sudden as the birds alighted, took flight, and the lawn was empty again.

Ouwinga carried on with the following grisly legend: "Well, it was back in the 1930s, long before you young twerps. (I looked around, thinking he aimed that at me and possibly some others in the area, when I noticed that only the five of us were there.) My father said that it happened on one of DeBoer's trucks. It was God's quick judgment, is what it was. The man must have had it coming."

I remembered my purpose for this visit, and began furiously to take notes when all of a sudden he stopped, looked me in the eye through his glasses, and said, "All that scribbling makes me nervous, young man."

"Sorry, Mr. Ouwinga. I'll just listen." I put my pad and pen down.

He seemed rather deliberate before returning to his narrative. "Well, again, it was back in the 30s, so my father knew all about it and he told me what happened. He said the crook had just broken into one of the nearby stores to burglarize it, and was nearly caught trying to get away. The fool almost walked right into the cops. At the last minute he saw them coming and tried to hide. He couldn't find any place to go; thought he was clever, mind you, and climbed up on the top of a garbage truck parked nearby. Not the cab, mind you, but right up on top the body. Well, I guess it worked for a while. The cops were scratching their heads; they couldn't find the man no way."

I observed the others were listening halfheartedly and conjectured they had heard this story a hundred times. But it was new to me and I listened intently.

Ouwinga continued, "Well, the crook probably thought he was going to get away when the DeBoer man got in and started to drive off."

Van Otten interjected, "The driver was Tom Dykstra. I remember that."

"Nope, it was his brudder Frank," corrected DeGraaf.

"That ain't right, Paul." Van Otten insisted. "You always get the two confused. Frank never worked on the truck. You're getting the two Dykstra families mixed up. That's a different Frank Dykstra; their family went to the Oak Park church, and the father …."

"Mr. Ouwinga," I jumped in, trying to be as polite as I could. I sensed the narrative getting lost in a morass of ethnic connections and family networks that were about to be chronicled. "So tell me. What happened in the story? The bad guy was hiding on top the truck?"

The two men took their cue and let Ouwinga continue.

"Well, can you imagine the look in the poor man's face when he sees the old viaduct over at Crawford and 31st coming up at him? Who knows, maybe he never saw what hit him. Anyhow, with a clearance of only four inches, there wasn't much left."

The four men continued to recount stories of misfortunes, some true, and some stretchers. Their narratives reminded me that many workers' arms, legs, and fingers have disappeared in the course of laboring in the refuse industry. From Ouwinga's point of view, most of the accidents came because of the foolishness of the men involved.

DeGraaf jumped to the defense of the common laborer. "Hey, man, you tell me why it took so long for Heil Truck to change da hoppers' way of goin' up and down, leaving dat open space underneath for guys to fall into and get a serious hurt. And why the Leach people couldn't get rid of dat complete cycle motion on their old trucks? If a man fell into the hopper and was by himself, it was all over but the crying."

He finished his diatribe with a sarcastic laugh, and red-faced by now, quickly became serious, his mouth almost cracking, his eyes showing hurt. "Dey didn't really try to make their trucks safer until a lotta good guys got hurt and dey got slapped wit some big lawsuits."

The other three nodded in varying degrees of agreement, but all four acknowledged that as long as the industry used machinery that cuts, compresses, grinds, and hauls the waste of society, there would be maiming and death.

Just then, the nursing attendant came by with some medication for both Riemersma and Van Otten. They grudgingly took the pills, and Riemersma squinted at me. "Young'un, enjoy your healt' vile you got it. Vatch what you eat and how much you trink." He spat on the ground.

I thought of that fourth slice of Bacino's pizza I had had the night before and felt reprimanded. "I will, Mr. Riemersma."

To steer the discussion onto a lighter vein, I shared with them my personal experience of seeing a fellow garbageman lose a wooden skid off the top of his load at sixty mph on the Stevenson Expressway. The heavy pallet slid harmlessly for a ways along the road and eventually off onto the shoulder, without serious consequences.

That brought some recollections. Van Otten began with the story of one hapless driver who hit a large pothole with his roll-off truck precisely at the moment when a Chicago police car was cruising right behind. Two boxes of assorted trash landed on the hood of the squad and surprised the dickens out of the cop.

Riemersma told of a time when a valuable piece of machinery worth thousands of dollars was placed too near the trash on the loading dock, the driver figured everything there was fair game, and sent a valuable piece of engineering to the landfill.

All four could recall many garbagemen who discovered that their loads were on fire because some fool had left hot coals in the can. If the driver was lucky, Van Otten pointed out, he would be able to quickly dump the entire truck's contents on some poor storeowner's parking lot and call the fire trucks. A few weren't so fortunate and the entire rig would go up in flames.

Riemersma got a kick out of something personal at that point, and began to chuckle inwardly. He spit into the grass and shared the following: "I remember it was on ta tird packer truck I eber worked on, in the fifties. I tidn't know ta pressure ta back blade had. Some man, he ask me to trow in some long slabs of steel, musta been fifteen feet if tey were an inch. How was I to know tat soon tey were to be poppin' out of te side, right trou' te tick wall of steel. Tat's te last time I eber put long pieces of metal in te truck. My boss made sure of tat!"

DeGraaf threw in the story of how one of his fellow drivers had driven his rig two miles through city traffic before the cops stopped him for littering. "Da guy forgot to close his tailgate on his roll-off, and was dropping rubbish all along North LaSalle. Man, my boss was hot." DeGraaf added, "He fired da fool dat same day." Ouwinga nodded, got a little red-faced, and I then remembered that DeGraaf had worked for him for many years.

Ouwinga turned serious. "Well, I once had a driver that cost me plenty until I finally wised up and fired him. The last straw was when he backed one of my brand new trucks into a compactor in the landfill. The big machine twisted the chassis into a pretzel." He hesitated and took a drink of water from a nearby glass. "I should've got rid of him months before."

By this time, it was obvious that Riemersma was trying to restrain himself, and couldn't any longer. He let loose with a great chuckle, "Didn't ya tink ya made a mistake giving te guy wit his history tat brand new truck ta drive?" Spit flew onto the lawn. Even DeGraaf had his hand over his mouth stifling a laugh.

The calamity contest was turning serious. Van Otten took center stage with an interesting tale. "You guys remember Fred Boer, when he fell asleep on the Eisenhower coming into town early one morning? He drove his truck right up the grassy embankment, through the fence, over the frontage street, into two more yards, and finally stopped when the sucker plowed into an apartment building near Paulina Avenue." At this point he checked both watches and examined the clock on the wall. Then he continued, as if he hadn't ever stopped. "Didn't hurt nobody, but many folks was sure rudely awakened, and was they ever mad."

Picturing a runaway truck going through the neighborhood even brought a smile to dour old Ouwinga. Riemersma squinted at me through those failing eyes of his, spat again, and began, "You guys remember te fellow who covered his

load perfectly, and ten, like a blinkin ijiot, forgot ta tie te tarp town? It wadn till te truck hit forty-five on te Eden's that it tecided to go flying, landin' on a car, coverin' it completely. The poor triver of te car, it was a lady, I tink, suddenly couldn't see nuttin, slammed on her brakes and swerved to a stop."

Riemersma was chuckling so hard that tears were streaming from his eyes. This was the medication he really needed. "No one was hurt, tank God. What I heard was, tat te driver kept on going, deciding ta pay for te new tarp ratter tan admit to his stupidity."

All four were shaking with laughter by this time. DeGraaf recalled gleefully the day one of the drivers for Leddenga & Sons was in a hurry leaving downtown. "Hey, man. You guys recall when Louis Hoekstra rolled his truck with a full load coming out of Lower Wacker? That was wild, man. The cars were all backed up behind, dey had nowhere to go, and da drivers couldn't tell what da hold up was. All the traffic coming out of da city was stalled for hours." DeGraaf was animated by now. "To make matters worse, Louis had done it just outside the tunnel; right in plain view of da guys wit the TV cameras. Aw, dose guys had a field day, man. Even the traffic copter got in some good ones. Leddenga didn't appreciate dat coverage, I can tell ya. Dey were bummed!"

That misfortune steered the men onto other public relations disasters. Riemersma shared the story of the hapless roll-off driver for Midtown Disposal who absentmindedly drove down a residential street for nearly a half-mile with his hoist upright, dragging down telephone lines in his wake. By the time a motorist made him aware of his error, many a telephone conversation came to a halt. The old Dutchman said that those who saw the Midtown truck harvesting the lines described the rig, draped with wire, as if it were a giant insect caught in some kind of spider's web. Riemersma took another spit and I finally moved over to sit with DeGraaf.

Van Otten then cleared his throat. The competition was heating up. He bragged, with a gleam in his eyes. "I can top that. Remember that one guy for Streelman, driving a box truck, who had the granddaddy of viaduct smashes? That sucker must have been motoring. The whole roll-off came flying off the truck's chassis when it hit the low bridge at Milwaukee and Grand. The box came to a total halt, the cable snapped, and the next minute it was on the ground." Van Otten was on a roll now, making sweeping gestures with his hands. "But the cab wanted to keep going west ... and it just went right up. For a split second, the driver saw the concrete ceiling up close and personal. Then he came back to earth with steel cables snapping, the roll-off box on its side and garbage all over the street."

DeGraaf's mouth was cracked wide, his eyes just slits, his face a picture of mirth. He slapped Riemersma on the back, causing the poor fellow to swallow his next mouthful rather than spit it out.

I glanced at old Jake Ouwinga. His puritanical demeanor was gone now, and I could tell that he was warming up to the subject. He had his glasses off and was wiping his eyes with his handkerchief. Yet, he had been waiting patiently to pull rank, and now the old scavenger proceeded to tell his story.

"Well, some of you guys remember Ben Van Zwieten. He was a good worker, he was, but always a little scatterbrained. He might forget his lunch one day and the next, one of his stops. Like the old saying—"the man would forget his head if it weren't tied on.""

He paused, replaced his spectacles, and took a drink of water. My curiosity was up.

"Well, one week I assigned Ben to drive my old dumper packer. Now he knew how to operate it cause he had done it many times before."

Riemersma noticed my quizzical look and jumped in. "Young'un, do you remember vat a tumper packer vas?"

I began to reply, but then stumbled out the chute. I could only recall trucks that would push out the garbage with large walls or blades of steel. A packer dumper seemed incongruous, and he noticed my confusion.

"I tought so. You never seen an old tumper packer, tid you?"

Before I could answer, he went on.

"Tey made tumper packers for a few years until te truck makers got wit te program and put in te front push-out blades." Riemersma pointed out. "To get the garbage out, te triver needed to raise te body to tump."

Van Otten chimed in. "Yea, and that heavy packing blade in the back made the weight of the truck really uneven. I can remember dumping and having my front end go up off the ground. Course, I wasn't in it at the time, I can tell you. I would be outside, next to the truck, running that lever, with my tailgate open, and going up and down with the body … kind of doing a dance with the rig, trying to shake everything until all the rubbish was out."

Ouwinga wanted center stage again and commanded it with a look at the others as if to say shut up, please! "Well, to see a large vehicle such as a garbage truck with its front going up and down may have been quite a sight," he said, "but for many of the drivers, it was old hat. Besides, this type of rocking and rolling was fine for the truck. They were made for it."

DeGraaf interjected. "Hey man, I remember hearing of one truck dat tipped over on its side in a landfill."

"One truck?" questioned Van Otten. "Man, where you been? That happened tons of times."

The others, as well, gave DeGraaf a look, as if to say don't get us sidetracked.

Ouwinga continued. "Well, the incinerator on Laramie was another story. Truckers had to dump their trash into a great yawning pit, sometimes as much as thirty feet below the surface of the pavement. No one had ever lost his truck into the pit, but it was always in the back of everyone's mind. There was a two-foot high curb to prevent anybody from backing up too far. And there were heavy chains set in concrete that drivers were supposed to secure to the front of their vehicles as a safeguard."

"Ya, tat's if you remember to use it," offered Riemersma.

"Or want to take da time," admitted DeGraaf.

I could sense a rise among the three other men, for this, I gathered, was a well-worn tale. DeGraaf especially was red-faced with merriment. "I love dis next part," he said.

Ouwinga knew he had an audience and spoke as if he were addressing the church body. "Well now, Ben had dumped at the incinerator a bunch of times, but one day, the blame fool, he says he just forgot to chain up. He backed up to the pit, loosened his clamps like normal, and well, then, I guess he got distracted by seeing the big crane coming down, taking the gulps of garbage and bringing them to the fire on the other side of the wall.

"So Ben goes ahead and opened his tailgate, and then raised the body. He told me only a few yards of waste fell into the pit. Ben admitted to me later that he had really packed that load tight; he said he didn't want to dump and have to go back up north for a few stops."

"You can't blame the boy for that, Ouwinga," offered Van Otten. "He was trying to save you fuel."

"He was taking a shortcut, is what he was doing," retorted the old man in the wheelchair. "Well, then Ben made his second mistake. He raised the body some more, and, when still nothing came out, he got in the truck and popped the clutch, trying to jerk it out. The load remained wedged in the front half. Well, the crane operator was watching all this happen. Apparently, just when Ben had backed up a bit to get another running start, the entire load slid back, the weight shifted and the truck reared up as it were a bucking bronco. Or a better comparison may be a sinking ship; cause it flipped up and over, in a backwards fashion, and sank into the sea of garbage in the pit."

Riemersma slapped his knee, DeGraaf was covering his mouth with his hand, and Van Otten was examining the grass, his entire body shaking with mirth.

Ouwinga persisted, trying to be serious, but I could see a slight smile breaking into his visage. "Well, Ben was lucky, if there is such a thing, that even though he was in the cab, he didn't get hurt, just shaken up, as his truck did its acrobatic maneuver and went down twenty feet into the yawning pit of refuse. That one cost me. I had to call for two tow trucks. Between them and the incinerator crane, we finally worked the rig out. Well, it proved to be quite the sight for all the men lucky enough to go to the incinerator that day. By the end of the week, the story went around the whole community of my disappearing truck.

"While it may have been true," he continued, "that the truck wasn't the newest in my garage, I wasn't ready to have it become trash quite yet. And if I was, well, I sure wouldn't use the Laramie incinerator—those people charged too much."

At that point, the three howled in acknowledgment and even Ouwinga was cracking up, his glasses slipping off his nose. This was a great finish to the afternoon. The attendants called to say that lunch was ready and my friends needed to say goodbye. As I found my way out of the retirement home, I could hear Riemersma and Van Otten flirting with the women residents, while Ouwinga challenged DeGraaf to a race down the hall.

As I approached my car in the parking lot, I could hear the cardinals trilling their spring song, and the warm breezes still carried the smell of the new cut grass. I could also hear the approach of a garbage truck as it worked its way up the street. Of course, I let my car idle for a while to watch. The operator could not have been more than twenty-five years of age. His in-and-out-of-the-cab movements were steady and furious. The truck was barely stopped when the man was already halfway out the door, his fast pace to the cans on the curb deliberate, even as sweat poured off his forehead. With a strong sweep of his arms, he grabbed two cans and in a fluid motion, had them in the hopper and emptied in a matter of seconds. Taking the two empty containers in one hand, the agile young man flipped the cycling handle with his other. Even as the blade began its descent to pack the garbage, the cans were back at the curb and the driver in the cab, foot on the pedal, shifting into gear, eager to devour the cans thirty feet ahead. It's a young man's job, for sure.

11
The Stench
1987

The development of innovations such as Dumpsters and roll-off containers in the 1940s and 1950s led to greater efficiency for waste management companies and more convenience for the average consumer. Unfortunately, such temporary holders of trash are often open to the public and available for evil uses. Who has not heard of a heart-wrenching "baby found in trash" story? Finding a human corpse or various body parts is one thing that every refuse hauler harbors in the back of his mind. When that occurs, the grisly details spread from worker to worker, from company to company.

* * *

The July day had to be the hottest of the year, I thought to myself, just as the weather forecast called for, hovering at 95°. It was late in the morning and the working conditions were making it downright miserable. With temperatures only cooling down to 77° by the time the sun started back up, what could I expect? My clothes clung to every inch of my body as I tarped a load of rubbish in a twenty-five yard rectangular container off the 800 block of North LaSalle Street. The city air was still, wrapped tightly around my throat, and I recalled the mushroom beds I helped place in stifling heat one day years ago. That was good for the mushrooms, I was told. However, I was no fungus growing in manure and I was saturated with perspiration.

The giant steel box, about the size of a car, was positioned alongside a construction site, one of the many in this city that knocks itself down and grows back up constantly. The faded blue, scarred, and dented box, just about shoulder high, had been filled with wiring and ceiling tiles and, although not a heavy load, would spread its contents along the road if I didn't cover it. I climbed up to the top of the load and gingerly stepped from solid spot to solid spot, always prepared to fall into a hole, sinking thigh deep into who knows what lay underneath. I maneuvered the "lightweight" nylon tarp over the load, tied the ends and sides down securely with rubber straps, and then clambered into the cab of the truck.

Now, I questioned, will it ride up onto the rails the way it's supposed to? Engaging the power takeoff, I pulled the handle to draw up tight the hardened cable that they said was able to haul 80,000 pounds. The cable tightened and the truck backed up when it felt its tug. Leaving the brakes off, I guided the box up and on, even as my rig seemed to slide right under the coming load. Well, that went smooth, I said to myself. I was sweating enough from the heat and didn't need the stress of a misaligned box to add to my miseries.

The knowledge that thousands in the city were fighting this muggy heat helped little. I didn't want to contemplate the office workers in their cocoons towering over me. A slight bitterness was building inside as I observed the tiny heads going about their business routine, many stories up in the Chicago sky. They lived in another world, one of cleanliness, order, and quiet. The back alley grime, the stress of the loading docks, and cacophony of the city street, plus today's heat—insufferable, oppressive, energy-sapping heat were all part of my world.

* * *

Here I was again, another summer, another several weeks on the truck. Try as I might, I couldn't get this job out of my blood. For the last few years I had taken classes toward my Masters, and having accomplished that, was now the proud owner of an advanced degree. Nevertheless, the pay for extra degrees in teaching didn't come close to comparing with the paychecks I could snatch by operating a garbage truck for those three months of the year.

Don't get me wrong, teaching was fun—perhaps better put, teaching was edifying. This was fun—perhaps better put, this was interesting. A world-away interesting. Down and dirty fascinating. No, I said to myself, no way could I—would I—do this for a living. However, for the summers of my life, when I was still young enough, and when employers of disposal companies asked me—who could say no?

* * *

It was now close to 10 AM, and Lake Street, just west of the Kennedy, was swarming with its dirty life. I shifted my twenty-ton, City Disposal roll-off rig through the maze of traffic after emptying my fourth container box of the day. My radio boss told me to head west on Lake after dumping my load, that he would let me know the address soon. "What was the address," I wanted to know. "Just get going," he answered.

Whatever!

Taxis, delivery vans, buses, meat trucks, and garbage trucks were going back and forth in the business of feeding, serving, maintaining, and cleaning the city. Drivers in eighteen wheelers just in from the wide-open cornfields of Iowa squirmed in their oversize cabs trying to negotiate their behemoths in the narrow confines of cars or trucks parked and double-parked on one of the busiest thoroughfares of the city. The steel pillars holding up the Elevated were there as well, placed at regular intervals along the road, some dented, some old and rusty, all somewhat frightening to a truck driver wary of anything that may leap out and get in the way of his vehicle. Along this stretch of commerce, men in white overcoats, in spite of the heat, trafficked in cold half-cuts of beef, frozen boxes of poultry or sides of lamb. Others were toting loads of flowers or sacks of vegetables. Though it was broad daylight, prostitutes brazenly strutted their bodies to drivers.

This was blue-collar Chicago, where the real work was done. This beehive of humanity had a philosophy of "move quickly, move often, and if you can't, then move out of the way, because others are waiting to move in behind you."

The grinding screech of metal on metal signaled an approaching El train as the two-way radio came to life in my cab. A truck in front of me stopped in the street and the driver jumped out to unload. "Base to 25, Base to 25 ...." the tinny speaker crackled at full volume.

I reached for the mike while I checked my mirrors, made a split second decision, and maneuvered into the other lane to pass. By then the roar of the train only ten feet overhead drowned all else, making conversation a lost cause for the next several moments. Three men in refrigerator coats cut in front, burdened down with frozen sides of meat.

I shouted back into the microphone as the sound passed by, "Repeat, base, El overhead, this is 25, repeat the message."

"Base ... 25 ... exchange that box for a Charlie ... at 1238 South Kostner. See the foreman on the job for the ticket. Goes to transfer."

"Charlie box ... exchange ... 1238 Kostner." I shouted into the black plastic in my hand, "transfer ... 10-4, base." And the dispatcher disappeared into radio outer space.

I knew the location, I assured myself, as I replaced the mike to its spot on the dash. I had been there just a week ago to drop off an empty 25-yarder. This might be the same one, I figured. Then again, the Charlie box I dropped off days ago could have been picked up, emptied, and refilled several times over. I stopped my rig, allowing a Gonnella Bread driver to back his bright red delivery van into a particularly tight spot. A few horns sounded behind me. I ignored them.

My thoughts returned to the job at hand. Okay, dispatcher Ed wants me to drop off this empty container at Kostner, pick up the full one and dump its contents back in the transfer station. But something told me I wasn't going to be able to just drop off the empty and pick up the full. I'd been there and recalled that there wasn't room for something that simple. I would probably have to temporarily drop my empty box on a street nearby, pick up the full one, drop that somewhere else for a few minutes, go back and pick up the empty, spot it where the full one had been, and then pick up the full one again and then go dump.

Bother! All this futzing' would bring in $400 for the company and $15 for me. That is at least how I calculated it. I calculated that this would take me about an hour to do the rigmarole of finding the box, pulling it out of there, and dumping it.

I maneuvered around a city truck and its crew blocking traffic as they examined a hole in the street, ignored a prostitute as she gave me the eye and, as I took a swig from my water jug, headed for the Kostner address.

I came up to the entrance of the alley and checked it out. I could see the box about a hundred feet down the alley, exactly where I had put one a week ago. My misgivings were right on; I couldn't drop off the empty next to the full one and accomplish this in two quick movements. Damn, I hated to "pick and drop," "pick and drop." I would get dirty crawling in the crap under the box, the cable seems to get heavier every time, and all that "in and out."

There was a shortcut, I knew. I could drag the full box out with a chain; just lug the heavy sucker down the alley. Others drivers did this, and even I had done it, on occasion. This procedure would probably work on this container, although I always felt a sense of guilt doing it. Maybe it was because of the horrific noise it made as I dragged the box weighing several tons or so. Or maybe it was the damage the box sometimes did to the surface of the alley. On the other hand, maybe it just seemed a lazy way of doing it. Hey, I reasoned, they provided the chains with the trucks. It must be OK, right? I took another drink of water and convinced myself.

I backed down the alley to within three feet of the full container. The 25-yarder had been there for several days, was overflowing, and needed a tarp. This load seemed to be a mix of construction debris and neighborhood trash. I figured it weighed maybe six tons—12,000 pounds of metal, wood, paper, and miscellaneous crap. In most situations, there was a wall or fence surrounding the roll-off, some kind of control over who put in and what was put in. This container was open to the public—not a good thing.

Rather quickly I detected this load had an odor about it that was a little unusual, stronger than most. There was the stench of something decomposing, not rotting food or household trash; that was common, and I didn't even take note of that anymore. No, this load had that horrible, rank odor of decomposing flesh. The high temperature that had penetrated Chicago the last few days was doing its job on *something* in that box.

Walking back and forth on the load to push the waste down in preparation for tarping was an altogether miserable job. The stench seeped upwards and enveloped me as I stepped and sank a foot or two on cardboard, paint cans, drywall, crumpled up newspapers, and conduit wiring.

I suddenly made an executive decision. This trip wasn't going to get tarped. It would "ride OK" back to the transfer station. I wasn't going on the highway, I reasoned; I wouldn't top 30 mph anyhow.

As I went back to the cab, my imagination of the contents in that load grew. I recalled the stories that I had heard, the tales that all garbios talked about and many downright dreaded—finding a body in the garbage they picked up. "It happens," the old-timers would say, as they sipped from their coffee cups, a leer in their eye. One of them would take a bite of his bacon, chew it with relish, and look at me with a wink; "It'll happen to you too, boy, if you stay on the truck long enough."

Whatever it was, somewhere in that box, it was putrefying by the hour. By now not only was I convinced that I had a body here—it was getting ripe and looking like a big piece of bacon.

But first things first. I had to get the container on the truck. Should I drag it out? It'll be a lot quicker, I rationalized; yea, the boss would approve of that. However, I reconsidered; it will make a thunderous noise. Maybe someone will call the office. The boss wouldn't approve of that. I studied the situation and argued with myself for a while. I never quite felt okay, doing this chain drag thing. Then I wondered—could a cop give me a ticket? But it was a fun thing to do, I admitted to myself, acting like I was a train engineer, pulling two heavy boxes down the alley, and kind of a challenge too.

That convinced me.

I put the truck in reverse and inched back to within two feet of the roll-off box. Climbing out of the cab, I reached into the tool box welded to the side of the truck's chassis, pulled out a twenty-foot chain that seemed to weigh a ton, and designed to pull a hundred times that in weight. Securely wrapping one end around the hook on the truck, I stooped down and attached the other end of the chain to the roll bar.

As I was getting back in the cab, the dispatcher on the radio was telling Unit # 33 to do an exchange at the Merchandise Mart; I tuned out the squawking black box. I slowly let out the clutch; the rig moved forward, the chain tightened, and the truck stopped abruptly. I looked around. Saw no one. That was good. Here goes, I thought.

Easing off the clutch as I raised the RPMs, my truck, carrying one box the way it should and dragging the other container with its six-ton load of rubbish it shouldn't, lurched forward. Amidst a howl of screeching steel on concrete and the roar of the diesel engine belching black exhaust, my train of metal, rubber, and refuse moved down the alley gaining in speed. In twenty seconds, the noise was over and the show was complete. The box was clear of the spot where the construction crew wanted the empty.

Relaxing the pressure on the chain, I hurriedly went back to unhook the box, reversed the hundred feet or so down the alley to drop the empty. Now that it was in position, I went to track down the supervisor on the job site, locating him on the second floor as he was shouting orders amid a racket of construction noise. I laughed to myself. I was worried about making noise? This whole city was one noise machine.

After getting the necessary paperwork signed, I returned to the truck, wheeled back to the full reeking box, connected my cable, and with relative ease, slid it up onto my truck. One last look in my mirrors told me that all was ready for the drive; I headed for the dump. Arriving at the transfer station, I was third in line, happy that I didn't have to uncover this load. I couldn't smell anything in the cab, but I pictured the odors wafting upward from my truck, and the decomposing body buried under some of that drywall. What will I find when I dump, I wondered.

My imagination went into high gear. The cops will be crawling all over the place, talking to me, my bosses, everybody. Maybe people will read about this one in the papers. Hey, that would be cool. Maybe I'll get my picture in the Trib. Then I thought about the corpse—what will the body look like when it comes out, and am I ready for that? Maybe it was in parts, like you read about sometime. Oops, back to reality—Dick in the loader signaled it was my turn to go in.

The old transfer station where we deposited our refuse had been spacious and satisfactory for its original purpose as a warehouse. When City Disposal bought it from Leddenga & Sons in the 1970s and modified the building, they added a pit into which open trailer trucks would back in and get loaded before heading to the landfills. Back then people marveled and wondered what the garbage industry was coming to.

However, what had once been considered state of the art was now insufficient. Six-wheeled, double-axle straight jobs had grown to become eighteen wheelers carrying 80,000 pounds of refuse. The metropolitan area grew exponentially in its ability to produce refuse. America's insatiable need for better ways to relieve itself continued. Customers kept clamoring for bigger containers and the manufacturers were eager to comply. With the big-scoop loaders maneuvering to fill the semis on the lower level, packer trucks and roll-off trucks dumping their loads on the upper level, and the concrete floor full to overflowing, the transfer station was confining at best. Adding the ever-present collection of copper, brass, aluminum, wire, batteries and other recyclables spewing out of barrels meant there wasn't a lot of room.

The noise level at the transfer was at the top of the scale. Equipment backing up emitted an incessant beep-beep-beep. The truck engines roared as their hydraulic hoists rose twenty feet or more to drop their loads. Debris smashed on the floor and rumbled to a halt yards from the truck. This orchestra of machinery and cacophony of noise combined to make the building fascinating to observe, yet unnerving to enter.

Constructed in the 1940s for a smaller generation of trucks, the lack of height to the ceiling had become a problem. Drivers new to the transfer station were convinced their rig was ready to bring the roof down. The operator of the loader, always pressed for time and space himself, would assure them, "No problem, buddy, you got at least a foot. Dump it and get out of here! Other trucks are waiting to get in."

Yet, though technically the ceiling may have been high enough, the doorway definitely was not. The clearance was eighteen feet, and from cracks showing in the brickwork, it was apparent that a driver or two had hit the wall in the past.

The usual procedure in the transfer station was to back in to where the loader directed and then go through a series of steps. I laughed to myself as I recalled the lessons on how to approach the station I received the first day I hauled for City Disposal. Cal DeJong was my mentor … gruff old Cal, who struck fear, I think, in the hearts of all the new guys at City. He was only five feet, six inches tall and about as much around, but he was stern in his warnings, trying to foster the fear of death, God and Satan all rolled into one biblical lesson. He had probably seen scores of guys like me, young know-nothings who thought they were the epitome of a driving ace, full of machismo, and eager to impress. Cal was a necessary constraint to remind the young bucks who reported to work every summer that they operated heavy and potentially deadly vehicles on the streets of the city.

"OK, Larry, first unhook your tailgate," Cal would instruct on one of my rookie outings. "Wait … did you forget to take off the tarp? Fool! Drive back out and take the tarp off before you dump!"

Duly reprimanded, I would be getting more nervous by the minute.

"Next step?" I questioned.

"Now you can unhook the tailgate. Be careful the gate doesn't burst open under pressure and knock you silly. I've seen that happen to young guys. Keep your eyes open for debris like two hundred pound rocks that may fall out and break your leg. And remember! Attach the safety chain of the tailgate to the other side of the body. Otherwise, the gate will swing around and hit the floor as you raise the load. Or worse—it'll break off."

I would swing the gate open; ready to leap into the air if as much as a pop can came my way.

"Now what, Cal?" I asked timidly.

"Get in the cab and back up to the pit, as close as you can get without going over the edge. Watch it! You go too far and you'll fall in, truck, person, and job all gone in one fell swoop. Now, Larry, if you feel you're ready, raise the hoist and let her fly."

The satisfying sound of sliding refuse, the resultant lurch forward of the truck and the accompanying cloud of dust and debris.

"That went out nice, didn't it, Cal?"

"All right, pull forward a few feet, lower your hoist, disengage the power takeoff, drive out and close the gate.

I lumbered out of the building, happy to have accomplished the feat and still be alive.

"Did you check inside the box to make sure everything came out before you lowered it?"

I lied "Yep. Now what, Cal?"

"Now that you're out of the garage, call the dispatcher on the radio and he'll tell you your next assignment."

"Thanks for the lesson, Cal. You're a good teacher."

"Aw, shut up!"

I was an asshole sometimes that first summer.

* * *

I put my truck in reverse, fighting the momentary blindness from the contrast of the bright sunlight with the dark recesses of the garage. Even as dust formed on my mirrors to obscure what little vision I had, I could now make out the back and forth movements of the loaders and other trucks dumping near the pit.

Cal's classes from summers ago just a dim memory, I focused on this load. Some trips to the transfer station promised treasures in the form of chewing gum still in the wrapper from Wrigley's, salvageable copper wire from Turner Construction, old Playboy magazines, or any of a number of things to make a driver's day. However, this load, I was convinced, promised a decaying human being and gruesome excitement.

With my truck in proper position, I climbed down out of the cab and, with gloves in hand, walked to the rear of the truck. A wretched odor came from this container, for sure. I released the tailgate and backed away quickly. I didn't want a bloody human head falling on my boots. To my disappointment the usual—a few boards, an empty bucket of drywall compound, some bent conduit, and a broken brick—spilled onto the floor. No dead body. Well ….. I didn't expect it to be that easy.

Back in the cab and with power takeoff in gear, I raised the hoist. Groaning from the weight it was expected to lift, then roared in response, the load sliding out in stages. It finished with a satisfactory whoosh and the truck lurched forward as the falling rubbish literally pushed the truck out of its way.

This payload went out cleanly, I could tell. My box was empty. Normally I would let the hoist down and drive out. Dick, the driver in the loader, would push the contents into the pit and that would be it. But I wasn't going to let this be normal. No way, I thought to myself, was I going to be denied the privilege of finding that body.

I leaped out of the cab and went back to the pile on the floor. At first glance, just construction debris. No load looked more typical than this one. So, I frowned, my box won't give up its dead! I kicked away some rags, yanked out a board, pushed over a piece of cardboard, and scavenged around for a full minute.

Dick was eyeing me, questioning what I was doing. I could read his mind. He's thinking about the other trucks that are waiting their turn, and wondering what the hell am I doing, wasting his time and everyone else's. He's probably saying to himself right now, "Get back in the truck, Larry, and pull that blasted truck out."

Feeling pressure and with a tad bit of disappointment, I did just that. I hopped into my cab and drove the truck out the door—with my hoist fully extended and the body all the way up!

With a sickening dull thud, the truck met the brick wall above the door and the 1940s construction began giving way. Horrific sounds followed. In seconds, my rig was engulfed with brick, wood, and dust. The doorway header came down on the roof of the cab; the windshield shot out in small pieces and both doors of the truck crumpled. Moments ago the passenger seat held my lunch box and water bottle; now there lay a one ton steel beam. If I had had a passenger that load, he would have been history. If I had driven two feet to my right, I would have been crushed in my own cab.

The dust was still settling as Dick and a few others cautiously approached. I think they expected a critically wounded, possibly dead driver. Instead, they saw an embarrassed young man looking back. I uttered a feeble "Sorry about that!" Unable to open either door, I squirmed out where the windshield had been and onto the hood of the truck.

Here was the wreck of the year. The cab was beyond repair. The doorway to the garage was in complete shambles. Going in or out this end of the station was impossible. The disruption to the company couldn't be greater. I had just ruined one truck and the entrance to the garage and was mortified.

The men asked if I was OK. I nodded sheepishly. Someone asked what I had been doing, digging around the pile like that for so long.

I told them of the odor I had smelled, my being convinced there had to be a rotting body in that load, and that was why I was looking. I mumbled something about being out of my normal routine and maybe that's why I drove the truck through the wall.

Dick, who had been around for many years and thought he had seen it all, said that the odor I smelled was probably dead rats rotting in the box, that it happens all the time in the heat of the summer. *Just dead rats.*

By this time, George Monsma, the foreman of City Disposal, had arrived on the scene. He wryly commented to me now that I understood the full stupidity of what I had just done, perhaps I should just go home for the day. Shake it off and come back tomorrow. Why my boss didn't throw me in the pit with the dead rats, drywall, and conduit, and send me off to the landfill as part of the day's refuse has puzzled me to this day.

12

Rat Tales

After working on the truck for a few summers, Christmas vacations and spring breaks, I became acquainted with the infamous rat tales making the rounds among old garbios. Over coffee and donuts at the mid-morning stop or after a couple of beers at the Friday afternoon gab session, the men would regale each other with gusto. They would expound on stories replete with rats of super size, rats being abnormally aggressive, rats that withstood several shovel-hits on the head only to walk away, seemingly unfazed, or of rats that outran the truck, as the driver, racing his rig down the alley, tried in vain to do them in.

Old-timers inform me that the rat infestation in the cities is considerably less now, due to modern sanitation methods and poison control. Legend was that the rodent problem was so bad in the 30s and 40s that the men resorted to tying their pants tight at the bottom with shoestring to keep the creatures from crawling up their legs.

* * *

Paul Ter Maat was a wizened old garbageman when he experienced his well-known run in with his rat friend, yet tough enough in his younger days to be able to empty two 55-gallon barrels from either side of his shoulder at one time, or so the story went. Paul and his partner, Jim DeBoer, were working—depending on the version one heard—in the alley behind the Palmer House, the lower level of the Wrigley Building, some run-of-the-mill greasy spoon on Wabash or on the South Side—the story has put him in all locations. Wherever, the rats were especially plentiful that year, so the two men had actually grown accustomed to the furry fuzz balls. Every rat was the same as far as the men were concerned; they simply wanted to help themselves to the garbage and were spooked when they heard or saw the garbageman coming. All a person had to do was to make noise or put on a light or shuffle some of the cans around and they got the message to hightail it out of there.

One night Ter Maat approached the garbage-strewn loading area and did the prescribed shifting and banging of cans. Several rats fled in their usual leap off the top of the can, a quick dart to a shadowy corner and then the disappearing act as they retreated to their warren of holes that lay under the alley's surface.

The barrels were positioned on a loading dock, a few feet above the pavement. Ter Maat, following usual procedure, would back up to a 55-gallon drum, grab it with one hand on the bottom, which would serve as a support, and position his other hand on the top of the container for control. Using his back to bear the hundred pounds plus load, the veteran garbageman would walk the twenty feet to the truck.

Having already emptied a few containers, Ter Maat grabbed the next and was halfway to the truck, when a rat leaped out from inside the drum, scurried down his arm and hung onto his pants leg. Not wanting to drop the barrel and make a mess, the man held on, even as he shook his leg with the animal still clinging for dear life. Ter Maat admitted later that if he had simply stood still, the rat probably would have left. However, you don't think clearly when a three-pound, mud-gray, hairy, red-eyed, bucktoothed rabies-carrying critter is clinging to your pants. Ter Maat kicked his leg up and out in an effort to rid himself of the clinging animal even as he was balancing one hundred pounds on his back.

It's not clear what possessed the rat to do its next move, but every garbio who has heard the story shakes his head with a grimace. Rather than taking a flying leap for the safety of some hole in the alley, this rodent saw an avenue of escape in the darkness inside Ter Maat's trousers. Before the poor man could react, the rat clambered to the first opening it saw and began to climb up his leg, sensing that wherever this long dark tight tunnel led to, it had to be safer than being out in the open with that scary man and noisy machine.

To Ter Maat's horror, he could see—and worse—feel the rat burrow slowly upward, getting closer to his groin by the second. The barrel fell to the pavement and cans and bottles went flying. In seconds, the animal was within striking range of his testicles. In a fit of terror mixed with rage, Ter Maat took the only recourse available. He grabbed at the lump that was traveling inside his thighs with both hands, all the while realizing that by doing so, the rat may bite the closest thing to it with his fierce teeth.

Ter Maat squashed the living, moving protuberance in his pants as tightly as his mighty muscles allowed, and the sound of a muffled screech could be heard through the fabric. The man was in a state of panic now, feeling something sharp, he thought, digging into his flesh. He screamed some words in Frisian just as partner DeBoer was coming upon the scene with his own barrel on his back. This was no time to stop the death grip now, Ter Maat knew. He squeezed even tighter, if that was possible, trying to pull the lump in his pants away from his leg. He could feel a warm liquid run down his leg and blood began to appear on his boot.

Not knowing if the flow of red was human or rat or a blend of both, Ter Maat kept the death stranglehold until there was no movement or noise. In a flash, he whipped off his belt and undid his pants, throwing modesty out the window. The crushed, lifeless body of a rat fell out and onto the ground, blood oozing out of the deformed mouth. Only superficial scratch marks remained on Ter Maat's inner thigh where the animal's claws had grasped for a grip in its death throes.

Shaken to the core, Ter Maat had no choice but to pull his trousers back on, though the animal's blood had soaked through the cloth. By now his partner DeBoer was quivering with silent laughter, but wisely keeping it to himself as best he could. He told Ter Maat to take a break and that he would finish the stop. Ter Maat sat down with a cigarette and uttered a quick prayer that his artery or worse hadn't been bitten.

Within weeks, the story of Paul Ter Maat and his traveling rat companion spread around the Dutch community. As usual, the rat grew in size and even number as the story made its rounds. Some wits suggested the rodent might have been female. This rat run-in was the impetus for a call for the city to literally wage all-out war against such pests. If we can control the Nazis and conquer back the Pacific from the Japanese, went the reasoning, could we not do a better job of cleaning the alleys?

Because the traditional approach of spreading rat poison throughout the city would be the main strategy, the argument always came back to how much toxin were we as citizens, and more importantly, the foodservice and transportation workers, willing to tolerate? When confronted with the possibility that every can of garbage slop and every box of refuse would be filled with a deadly cure, most of the garbagemen agreed to take matters into their own hands. *Just be more cautious* became the motto for all the scavengers: always wear thick gloves, rough clothing with Paul's incident in mind, remember to tie the pants legs with string. Henceforth, going 'Ter Maat' became the fashion statement for all garbios.

* * *

I'd heard the Ter Maat story is the standard for rat tales. But with thousands, possibly millions of rats gnawing their way under and around the city, interesting meetings between man and rodent are common. And like fish, rats tend to grow in stature if a storyteller needs extra punch to impress the others. I was made very aware of this one day after visiting my old trash-hauling friends at the local retirement center. Paul DeGraaf, Teunis Riemersma, John Van Otten, and Jake Ouwinga were there. Cal Pettinga, who also spent time on the truck and was relatively new to the Center, joined us. The five of them got into a rat-telling challenge and I was all ears.

When I arrived that Thursday afternoon in June, the gentlemen had had their lunch and were working on what might have been their fifth or sixth cup of coffee for the day. They were ribbing each other good-naturedly regarding their loyalties to the Cubs or White Sox, although both teams were close to the cellar and it was still early in the season. DeGraaf and Pettinga were in the minority as Southside fans, but the two were not about to back down. I discreetly sat down with the five men in the Cicero lounge, picking one of the soft recliners, admiring the plush feel.

The west and south walls were covered with knickknack shelves, holding an eclectic grouping of antique-looking items, early black and white photographs of Chicago neighborhoods and every monthly edition of The Reader's Digest and National Geographic published in the last fifteen years. The east wall of the room was a floor to ceiling bookcase holding an impressive collection of classical, philosophical, and theological books. I couldn't help but wonder if any of these residents would ever avail themselves of the many sources of information within easy reach. At this point in their lives, I speculated, earthly wisdom must seem rather fleeting.

Surrounded by this library setting, with the temperature in the room hovering at 75° and my body sinking luxuriously into the sense of age all around me, I could easily have nodded off as I listened to the men harangue each other over statistics, fan base, championships, and the like. There is definitely a somnolent air about a retirement home.

I was brought back to the land of the awake when a shriek, accompanied by several howls of "mouse, a mouse" came bolting out of the kitchen, just down the hallway. A rustling of footsteps, some violent opening and closing of cabinet doors followed, and soon a return to the normal muted hum of the ventilation system.

The men looked at each other and Van Otten was the first to give his opinion. Lately his choice of words could, on occasion, be a little coarse. "I think one of young women saw one of our *#*'friends, the little guy I saw the other day. I was gonna mention it to somebody, but forgot. Not that it woulda done any good."

"Ya got dat right, John!" DeGraaf replied. "It's one ting to see 'em, quite a bit else to get one o 'em. Anyhow, da ones around here is so small; dey can get into a hole da size of a quarter. Dey really ain't dat bad. It's not like dey're rats or something." DeGraaf's heavy Chicago slang had not diminished with age and only had increased, if anything.

"Ya, I vonder wat some of tese ladies would do if tey was to see a rat," Riemersma quipped in his Dutch accent, "like what we used to see down in Chicago by te railroad tracks or down by te river. Now dere is some chunk of rodent for ya."

"Ah, you remember the rats when we was young, men?" reminisced Pettinga, in one of his rare statements. "I don't think the city is bad now at all, not like I remember." Pettinga, the quietest of the group and eighty-eight years of age, seemed to understand fully the conversation, but was content to sit back and let the others do the talking.

DeGraaf continued "Man, dat year of 23 was the worst I remember, for the Cub's pitching—and the rats." He smiled at the three Cub loyalists, pleased with himself that he was able to get in one more dig. "Dat winter, it was way too mild, hardly no snow and never got down below zero. I tell ya, man, by de middle of dat summer, when the Cubs were in last place and the second batch of rat babies arrived, the numbers of dose animals was so bad dat, as we drove our old Reliable tru' the alleys, we could see the rodents by da hundreds—hundreds, I tell ya."

"That must have been the summer we would find the varmints living in our trucks, often pouring out of the hopper as the cycling blade was going." Van Otten volunteered. "We finally figured out that some of our rigs had nests right in the corners where the garbage collected. Didn't take us long to clean those out, I tell ya."

"Ya ain't remembering right, John." Riemersma interjected. "Trucks tidn't have compacting cycles 'til the forties. But I 'member hearing, I'm not lying now, about some barrels on some guy's route literally shaking from te large number of rats in 'em."

"Well, you probably saw that on my route," Ouwinga offered. His preferred posture throughout life was sitting ramrod straight in any setting, and while his advanced age and physical deterioration had relegated him to a wheelchair, he still had markedly good bearing, in spite of wearing thick-lens bifocals, giving the appearance that he was on his way to a Church council meeting. His tone of voice was, of the five, the most regal as well. "Some of my men once swore that one barrel was actually being carried away by the little creatures before my drivers grabbed it back from them."

DeGraaf nodded and added, "I tell ya, man, we had some on our route so fierce dat they would actual hiss back at ya when ya got 'em cornered."

"Tat ain't nottin'. I can beat all a' you on te power of te little beasts." Riemersma challenged. "We had one peculiar rat at a stop on South Clark tat, try as we might, we could not corner, poison, run over, or in any way kill it. Week after week, he eyed us from his hole overlooking te Chicago River. He got bigger and bigger until we sent in a team o' ten men to corner and finally smash him wit shovels." Riemersma finished with a flourish of his arms, acting as though he was wielding his own scoop, spitting into the nearby wastebasket for good measure.

Van Otten rose to the challenge. "Ha! Yea, well, on our route, we once had one rat so goldurn big that when Ronnie DeVries—you guys remember

Ronnie—when Ronnie went after him with his shovel, the animal grabbed it right out of his hands … and started swinging it back at him. DeVries had to go pull his gun out of the truck to kill the sucker."

A collection of oohs and aahs followed that one. DeGraaf appeared a little indignant, feeling that he didn't impress the others enough. "None of ya guys can top what we had once. One of our men actually had to run back into da truck and close da door; da rats was so vicious. He drove out of dat alley, pell mell, and da wheels slipping and sliding on rat bodies all the way. Said dat was the reason he hit da side of the building that day."

Pettinga and Riemersma rolled their eyes and smirked a little.

By this point, Ouwinga's cheeks were getting a little flushed. "Well, yes—that's all fine and well. But have any of you heard what happened to old Thomas VanDyken who worked for us?" (They hadn't, or if they did, wanted to hear the story again.) He went on, "Well, it happened one winter night, when it was really quite cold. He had been picking up under Michigan Avenue, by the Billy Goat, and had been seeing some rather large rodents in that alley for weeks. We had complained to the city, mind you, but you know how well the city works. They said they sent out their crews that supposedly did some poisoning.

"Well, it wasn't working, I can tell you that. Well, this is according to old VanDyken, but he said that as he was getting the barrels up from the basement, by the time he got back to the truck, it was moving! Yes, I kid you not; the vehicle was slowly going down the alley, apparently being taken over by the rats themselves. Well, he dropped the one barrel he had on his back, ran up to the truck, and jumped on the running board to look inside. Lo and behold, now this is what Tom said, and I never had cause to doubt the man, he swore he saw two rats trying to steer the wheel, one operating the gas, one working the clutch and three trying to shift it into second."

They all howled at that one and even Ouwinga betrayed a little grin. The four slowly grew quiet however, when they noticed that Pettinga wasn't getting into the mood for some reason, and hadn't said a word for quite some time. One of the men pointed this out and asked what the problem was.

Pettinga replied quietly, "Gentlemen, you know I've been in the business as long as any of you." He glanced at each and then averted his gaze to the floor.

They all nodded their assent. Their eyes told him to go on.

"It just that the mere thought of what I remember … is too hard to get out," Pettinga murmured softly, "It causes me nightmares whenever I think of it. I would just as soon forget it ever occurred." The slight tremor in his voice and that last phrase, spoken with such a hushed tone, brought the whole room to attention. The men, of course, had known Cal for years, but apparently had never heard of the terrible, dark secret that he kept in his heart. They pleaded, begged, and admonished him to share the story. After several minutes of such prodding, he finally relented.

"It was the fall of 1946 on the west side of Clinton Street, between Randolph and Washington." Pettinga began. "That whole block was mine, you may recall, many years ago."

Ouwinga and Van Otten nodded, feeling a little uneasy. In the nineteen fifties, between the two of them, they had gobbled up that whole street from Lake to Van Buren. But that was years after the incident that Pettinga was about to share.

He continued, "That was the summer we had some of those super rats, critters so large and so strong, that they would eat anything the restaurants on Clinton put out. Day after day, by the time my men and I got there, these monstrous rats had beaten us to the garbage. The lids were torn off, the contents scarfed out and completely consumed. Any type of food, bones, paper, even the tin cans, everything. All that was left were the stark empty cans. It was horrifying." Pettinga's eyes were wide now and he was gesturing with his hands.

Riemersma and Ouwinga both swallowed hard. Van Otten inadvertently checked under the chair he was on. DeGraaf had a peculiar pale look and his eyes were beginning to water.

Pettinga continued, in his slow, interminable way. "That was not all, gentlemen. Worse was to come. In fact, one day the most terrifying thing happened."

As the four aged men leaned over to soak in this tale of terror, Pettinga spoke in an increasingly muted hush. He knew he had them and was working for the greatest affect. "Early one day, as I wandered down the alley, searching in vain for any trace of the vicious rodents who were menacing my stops so much, the owners of the restaurants came out to present the bad news."

"What?" the four whispered in unison. Visions of garbagemen, stricken with rabies, foaming at the mouth and running through the streets flashed before their eyes. Van Otten pictured the half-eaten remains of a worker lying on a dock.

Pettinga continued. "The restaurant owners had had a meeting about the situation. They were aware that the rats were out of control, and that the animals were eating all the garbage that they were putting out before my men could even get to it. So they came to a decision, although it was extremely hard for them to get it out." He paused.

"Go on," yelled DeGraaf.

"You ton't mean..!" shrieked Riemersma.

"No, I don't want to hear it!" moaned Ouwinga.

Van Otten by now was grasping at his throat as if for air and whispering a string of expletives.

"Yes, it's true." Pettinga muttered almost inaudibly. "They said that on account of the rats, they didn't need me or my business any more. The animals were more efficient, more reliable, and quieter to boot. They were ending their accounts with me. What could I say? I staggered out of the alley in a daze...and I lost all my business in that whole block—$700 every week."

I heard the sound of falling bodies and collapsing chairs. The four Wooden Shoes fainted as if one. As I called for the nurses to come to their aid and bring them away, Pettinga remained strangely calm, with a slight smile on his lips and a twinkle in his eyes.

I was later informed that the Center's head nurse gave the order—in the future, the staff were to carefully monitor all story-telling sessions. Really frightening topics, such as losing money, were strictly verboten.

13

In the Bowels of the City

1990

"Unit 23—Base here." The speaker blasted out the words in a scratchy fashion. I grabbed for the finger-worn mike attached to the dash as I blissfully sailed through the stoplights on Randolph. Driving in the Loop at 4:30 a.m. is pure luxury, I was thinking. "If you've dropped your empty at 333 Wacker, head to the Mart. You're after a 20-yarder, in the cave."

"Roger." I shouted back, eager to affirm that I had heard the message and glad that I, by accident, was heading in the right direction.

A moment of silence from the little black box hanging from the ceiling in my cab.

"Unit 23?"

"Yes, Base?"

"Aren't you going to ask which slot? … Hey, wait a minute … you ever been there? Which street are you gonna take?"

"Uh … I don't know. The Mart's by the river. Can't miss it. I think I'll take Wells, I guess." As soon as the words left my mouth, I knew it wasn't the right answer. "Why?" I asked the mike, "Which one am I supposed to take?"

Another moment of silence, uncomfortably long.

"Look, 23, you're not going there in your car, remember. And you're not going shopping. You been to the cave?"

"To a cave? Yea, sure. I've been to some caves. Been to Mammoth Cave, Cave of the Ozarks and …."

"Look, Unit 23," thundered the voice from base. "I'm not in the %*# mood. I mean the cave, where we keep our containers, under the Merchandise Mart."

"The what?" I threw my question back into the black piece of plastic in my hand, now sure something was wrong.

"Just as I thought." … a long pause …."summer idiot." … another pause and apparently some thinking going on back at base. "You ain't been there, have you? I wondered if I'd sent you. The other dispatchers haven't either, apparently."

By now, I had double-parked on Wells Street as close to the side as I dared without taking off a few car fenders. I put on my flashers and applied the air brake. I had been on the road for 30 minutes—max. Yet, I could tell another adventure was coming and this radio discussion needed my complete attention.

"OK, Base. I'm parked, got pen and paper, and ready for directions."

The crackly voice was hesitant. "You ain't ever been there …." he repeated. The idea seemed hard for the man to digest. " … I can't give you @&*% directions to that place over the radio …." Another pause …. more thinking. " … Gol' dang it. I ain't got anybody else in the area right now, either." I could almost hear his brain grinding. "Unit 23, I'll walk you through it; that's what I'll do. Head for LaSalle Street, going north. When you're over the river, get back to me."

"Ten four, Base." I gladly jammed the mike back in its cradle, happy to quit this pleasant conversation. Dispatcher Ken didn't like me—that was obvious. What I ever did to him was a mystery. Heck, we hadn't seen each other for nine months. But perhaps that was simply it. I was just a part-timer and did not quite qualify in his mind.

This was my third stint for the garbage-hauling firm of City Services. Each season I was learning more of their vast repertoire of stops throughout the metropolitan area. And by my reckoning, this was my twelfth summer on the garbage truck, spread out over some thirty years of being a student, then teacher. Now that I was back in the saddle, I could see that things were changing in this business. I had worked one summer for this same company back in the 1970s when it was known as Leddenga Scavenger. Since then, it had grown to become a citywide behemoth that employed hundreds. When the Leddengas sold out to a conglomerate known as City Disposal, the family members stayed with the company for a time. Now, with the exception of two great grandsons employed in some suburban office building, no Leddenga remained in the business. In fact, it was only through two longtime drivers and a manager that I was able to get this job as vacation help. Their office was eager to oblige when they realized it was cheaper to employ me at a non-union rate than paying overtime to a regular.

Two years ago this corporation tried to shed its Neanderthal image and words such as scavenger and disposal; and opted to be called City Services and Recycling. Now that they were such a modern corporation, they tried to fool the public into thinking that all the rubbish they picked up was magically recycled into paper, food and 100% oxygen.

Such glory in the garbage-hauling business!

Somewhere along the way, we drivers lost our names as well, it now being policy to call us by our truck number. That, and the fact that we were required to weigh in at the scale before and after every load, record every move in our log books, and were terminated if we were caught keeping any item found in the trash, combined to make this job more onerous.

Sure, I told myself, the trucks now had FM band radios with tape decks, air conditioned cabs, nice paint jobs, and fully synchronized transmissions. And yes, we were all issued crisp uniforms, the old garage had been renovated, and a lunchroom installed. But, I wondered, was I just becoming an old romantic, looking back with a rose-tinted vision of the good old days? It was obvious that the old ways were surely disappearing, and I could sense from several veterans their frustrations as well.

For a few years after the Leddenga buyout, many of the trucks still carried the family name on the doors, though in smaller print. Nevertheless, by 1990, the Leddenga ticket books, Leddenga container decals and Leddenga jackets had long disappeared. Now it was called City Services & Recycling, as generic a name as one could come up with.

Indeed, from what I could gather, very few of the workers knew the company's history, let alone had ever met one of the Leddengas. To the men who pulled out of his old buildings on Halsted, Sam Leddenga, the old wooden shoe founder of the business, was as remote as George Washington or Abe Lincoln.

Sam, the firstborn son of a Dutch immigrant, had worked the streets of the city at the turn of the century with his team of horses, and had only purchased his first truck, a Diamond Reo, in 1926. His three sons carried on—expanding the business, investing in a larger garage, buying farmland out west for dumping—and were among the first haulers in Chicago to use hydraulic packers. For decades, trucks bearing the name *Sam Leddenga & Sons, Scavengers* crawled through the alleys and streets of downtown Chicago. Many buildings displayed the official markers advertising to anyone who might wonder that this stop was the domain of Sam and his family. However, by now all such signs of Leddenga Scavenger were in the trash-heap of the past.

I knew this is the way of Chicago—constantly redoing itself. Like the hated S Curve on Lake Shore Drive, the odorous Chicago stockyards, or the red lip Magi-Kist billboards, the old businesses, ways, and men were swept aside, buried, and forgotten.

I wasn't in that category yet, but for the first time, I could sense it coming. Dispatcher Ken was at least ten years my junior. Getting orders from a younger source was unnerving.

In all the summers I had driven for Leddenga Scavenger/City Disposal/City Services & Recycling, I had never been sent to the lower level of the Merchandise Mart. I gathered that where I was headed now, was not the Mart that most know. I had the gut feeling that I was to go down deep, to its literal foundation. Driving north on LaSalle, over the river, I observed the massive structure on my left. The Merchandise Mart was a mammoth edifice to commercialism; created by Marshall Field in 1930, purchased later by Kennedy wealth, it was now a showcase of clothes, furniture, and other durable goods.

Crossing over the still dark Chicago River with the lights of the city sparkling on the water's surface, I picked up the mike and called my friend Ken. "Base, this is 23 … on LaSalle. Over."

The speaker-box came to life. "Unit 23, listen carefully now. I'm going to talk you through this, right down to the cave. We got three boxes there, ya hear. But don't get the idea that there's a lot of room." Ken's sense of importance was growing by the second. "Rather tight down in the cave; that's why we call it the cave. Got that?"

Sarcasm dripped out of the speaker and landed on the floor next to me. "Yes, base," I replied, "I'm all ears."

"Turn right on Kinzie and go about a hundred feet. First right you see, turn again. They built a little alleyway under the Mart years ago. That's where you're headed. With me?"

"Right, then another right." I repeated, and hung up the 'phone'.

I turned, lumbered down a block, and turned right again. I said goodbye to the city as I began my descent, the walls of the LaSalle Street Bridge arching over and on either side of me. As I began my trip into this netherworld, I figured I would not see the sky again for a while. The concrete surface underneath my truck had deteriorated to gravel.

A few aging lights on the walls tried to penetrate the gloom, but their efforts failed miserably. My headlights shot dusty beams into the growing gray. *Somewhere down here is a loading area*, I thought to myself. *Can't be that hard to find.*

Soon the wall of concrete on my left opened to indicate a truck dock, and I turned in, grabbing the mike. "Base—unit 23. I see the dock on my left. Is that where I'm going?"

"Nah, you got a long ways to go yet. That's for the delivery trucks, the eighteen wheelers, and such. Keeping the dock on your left, head back south, toward the river. You're going to find a little roadway running along the water. Can you see the river up ahead? Over."

The surface below my tires had now deteriorated into dirt mixed with gravel. I was in a dark and down world, heading back in time. The area was rather wide, but with a height of perhaps only fourteen feet. Rows and rows of concrete beams held up the massive ceiling of the cavernous loading dock, each bearing the scars of attacks by trucks over many years. Gouges marked with various colors indicated that drivers had unsuccessfully maneuvered their vehicles around the supports. The thought struck me that a few key beams, hit by an out-of-control truck, could fail, and the Mart, one of the larger structures in the world, would collapse. My truck and I would never be found.

I continued my southerly direction now at a crawl, seeing off in the distance a grayish hue that appeared to be a wall. In a few moments, the barrier in question drew near and I realized it was the river itself. Just as I was convinced my route had hit a dead-end, the track I was following veered again to the left, and dutifully, I turned.

"Unit 23 to base. I'm heading east again. How far up ahead is this cave?"

"You got a ways to go, 23." He repeated, almost chuckling. "On your right is the water, to your left, an old dock that they don't use anymore. Am I correct?"

"Ten-four."

"Getting kind of tight down there, 23?"

"Correcto', base. I take it there's room to turn around at the end? This would be a long ways to back up."

"You'll have room, 23. You will need to do some maneuvering, but the others do it."

Feeling pressure now from several directions, I continued traveling parallel to and barely two feet above the Chicago River, separated by an old concrete and brick rampart that showed cracks and a few gaping holes. The path I was on—it couldn't be called a road by any stretch—was barely wide enough for my rig to navigate. I plunged ahead, because I knew others had done so, and Dispatcher Ken said to.

On my left, pillars by the score, coated with city grime, and the occasional graffiti. Faintly visible in the gloom of the early morning dawn and almost obscured by the forest of concrete trees, appeared twenty or more loading docks, all worn from age and use, seemingly abandoned by the newer, larger trucks. On my right, the wall of old mortar and stone that kept the dark Chicago River and me apart. Above, aging iron beams, encrusted with decades of pigeon droppings and remains of nests. I gathered that this was not on the list of must-see sights for the city Bureau of Tourism.

Where was my guiding voice sending me, I wondered? I'm to pick up a container box down here? How would that be possible? I observed that the ceiling had now dwindled to a height of not more than eleven feet. Where would I turn around? How would I raise my hoist? One of the cardinal rules of driving truck is to never get into a position that you can't back out of. Yet here I was, plummeting straight into a hole. For reassurance, I reached for the mike.

Ken must have read my mind, because before I could press the button, "Keep going straight," came squawking out of the box.

I returned the mike to the cradle, feeling admonished for my lack of faith, and kept the truck moving at a slow idle. In the murky distance, another wall was looming larger. My truck and I had become a mole, burrowing further into the under city.

Fifty yards to the wall … The river on my right …. ancient columns on my left …. Ceiling almost scraping my cab …. Thirty yards …. I will follow his directions explicitly. I'll just hit the wall at five mph. It won't hurt the truck or me. That'll show him.

Just when I could see no possibility of continuing …. there, in the shadows, a cavity appeared on the left side. Since I left the city lights and open sky, I had done a full 360°. Every time I was about to hit a dead end, there appeared another hole for my truck to wiggle into. With no recourse but to follow my nose, I swung my truck and, like before, there was just enough room to clear the supports. Someone years ago had planned this route for a truck of this size and not one foot longer.

And there, ten yards distant, illuminated by my headlights, appeared a wall of steel. My progress was finally at an end. I recalled Tom Sawyer and his misadventure in a cavern along the Mississippi. By now I was surrounded by massive wooden beams, more logs than lumber. I pictured the builders of the Mart harvesting these immense old oaks from the ruins of Fort Dearborn and delivering them to this spot. The ceiling of the Mart had dwindled to one foot higher than my cab. A feeling of claustrophobia began to creep upon me. I felt a kinship with the mummies of Egypt.

"Unit 23 to base." I whispered, so as to not wake the dead. "Can you hear me down hear?"

"Loud and clear, 23. Did you find the door yet?"

At that precise moment, the wall became a door and began to rise. An ugly, yellow glare fell upon soil that had not seen daylight or rain since construction of the Mart. The wall/door continued its ascent to reveal yet another passageway. In the low light, I detected three well-used Leddenga-now-become-City Service roll-off containers. On the concrete landing stood a security guard who had just pushed the magic button. I found myself where no tourists and very few Chicagoans ever get, yet alone know exist. I was duly impressed.

"Base, you're the man … I'm here! Hey—how did they know to open the door just when I pulled up?"

"I have one of these new things called a phone, Unit 23. Wonderful invention, the phone." More drips on my floor.

Grudgingly, I had to admit Dispatcher Ken was right. There was room to make a tight turn. Thankful for power steering, I finagled my truck around and began to cable up. Bringing the box up on the rails proved uneventful, with the hoist and the box clearing the ceiling by a full two inches. From the telling gashes in the ceiling supports, it was obvious other drivers weren't as fortunate.

As the guard was signing the ticket, a fellow City truck came lumbering in to my little world. His entrance was marked by a swift sure approach and a cloud of dust, the sign of an experienced traveler in this tight confine. This truck and the guy driving it was Unit 17, a vaguely familiar face from past summers, and from appearances, a man in his late fifties. The massive build of his torso and wrinkled gray hair was striking. I figured the driver had a name, but recalling the new company policy, couldn't verify that. He was delivering an empty box to the slot where I had just pulled the full.

We conversed for a short while on the narrowness of our world here and the right and wrong ways of working in such a small space. I figured he had this cave thing down pat. "It looked like you could do that last turn in your sleep, 17. Been down here many times, I take it?"

"Yea, dey send me to the cave a lot, cause I'm good at dis place. Yet, I tell ya, man, I always feels da butterflies when I'm down here. Near as I unnerstan, they only send four or five guys." He laughed a deep chuckle. "You should feel good, 23, dat dey even thinks you can handle it." He paused and thought a bit. "Hey, man—maybe dis summer dey gonna send you here more and me less." That seemed to tickle his funny bone, and he let out a good laugh.

"How long you been with City?" I asked.

"Long time, man. I was here way back when dis was called Leddenga." He proudly pointed out. "Dat's long time ago!"

"So you knew that City Services used to be Leddenga Scavenger," I marveled. "I didn't think any of the workers here lasted any longer than five years. Did you ever meet John Leddenga or his brothers?"

"Hey, 23. Cut me some slack. Dis is my thirty-third year. I'm an old garbio. Seen many guys come and go. I seen the Leddengas go as well. I knew the brothers. John was okay, so was Bill, sometimes. Me? I got along with Ralph, the best. He hired me, one of the first blacks to work for the company. I always appreciated that."

"Hey," I exclaimed, breaking all protocol, "I think I remember you from when I worked for Leddengas in college. What's your name?"

He looked around. "I'm Arthur, but don't tell the base I told you that!" and we both laughed.

I shared with him that I had worked for the company one summer back in 1970. It struck us both, then, that we had known each other once before, separated by a span of 20 years. A bond, the tie of age, drew us together.

"Hey, 23." His aging dark eyes glittered. "I bet you'll be interested in seeing something over here, something older than bot' you and me." And he headed to a far corner of the loading area, motioning that I should follow him.

My curiosity was up, and I followed him warily, "What's that, Arthur, I mean, 17? What you got over there?" I wondered if he had committed the unpardonable sin and stashed some old brass or copper piping in a hiding place.

He approached the wall nearest the door and carefully scanned the surface in the dim light of our truck's beams. "It's been years since I last seen it, but I think it's over here somewhere … I don't think anybody would take it down …." He was talking to the old wooden supports as much as to me, scraping the old grime away with his gloves. "Not too many knew it was even here. C'mon now fella … where are you?"

Arthur/17 continued rubbing at the age-encrusted walls, as we stood some sixty feet below the city street. Within a minute, however, he turned to me smiling and proudly pointed at a small tin plate bolted to one of the supports.

"Ain't that something for the museums, 23?"

With several swipes of my glove, I could make out the words *Samuel Leddenga, Scavenger—Telephone Olympic 2-5647.*

"There, told you that it was down here somewhere. Dis thing is old, 23."

I did some quick math. "Some fifty years, if it's a day!"

We looked at each other, then back at the small 4 by 6-inch metal emblem.

At that moment, time stood still. The rumble of the cars and trucks above us, even at this early hour, was an annoying backdrop. I pictured Sam Leddenga bolting that plaque to the wall more than half a century ago as he claimed the massive new Merchandise Mart his territory, hoping to build his company based on its commerce. Hundreds, no, thousands of times he, his sons, and his workers ventured down into the cave to bring forth the trash and garbage. This trek might have been an arduous journey, but it must have been sweet to their bank account as well. The stop was still making money decades later.

I soon said goodbye to my reacquainted friend and, minutes later, found myself in the glow of the newly risen sun on LaSalle Street. I was feeling good about myself now, for I was a veteran of the cave and figured I wouldn't mind taking that trip again. I grabbed for the mike, "Unit 23 to base. Coming in with the box from the left slot. Found it with no problem. Got out of there without scraping my head on the ceiling as well."

I thought a second; then added, "Hey, I like the cave, base. Wouldn't mind going there in the future. "

"Base to 23. Yea, well, forget about it. Haven't you read the papers? They're doing a major renovation at the Mart, starting this summer. In a week or two, that whole area going be all torn up and cleaned out. Everything down there going into the landfill. About time, too. Nothing but worthless old stuff. "

"Ten-four, base."

14

Show Time

1991

"Rich and poor have this in common:
The Lord is the Maker of them all."
—PROVERBS 22:2

My truck's exhaust stack belched out a black/gray plume; the diesel engine roared its agreement. Together this was enough to persuade the truck's cable to pull the front of the 50,000 lb. container two feet off the ground. Two feet! But that was all it could manage, even while lifting my cab a frustrating equal distance off the surface of the street. We remained there for a while in a truck versus container tug-a-war, neither one admitting defeat. I was at the steering wheel of four tons of manly machinery, looking down from lofty heights, my truck's chrome stacks and bumpers shining. The noise of the pistons roaring through the canyons of the urban jungle showed to anyone stopping to stare that I was in command of a powerful tool. Yet, it was becoming obvious it was not authoritative enough to do its job. I was embarrassed for my friend Mack—it had failed me and was showing its impotency to all of Chicago.

* * *

This was my third summer driving for City Disposal, now called City Services & Recycling. I was assigned to a refuse-hauling truck designated by some in the industry as a roll-off container truck and by others a box truck. Whatever one calls it, its purpose is to pick up containers filled with refuse of all types. These objects of my attraction were scattered around the city, in alleys and at docks, in the Loop and in outlying areas serving homes and industry. Containers ranged from 7 yards to mammoths of 50+, containing bricks, paper, metal, or pure slop. A few of the hundreds scattered around the city were new; but the vast majority were beaten and mangled things abused by customers and drivers alike. No one cared about a roll-off container. On occasion a box would fight back in the only way possible, as if to show that it understood its lowly place in the universe.

Cooperation meant rising up, straight and true, locked onto the rails of the truck. One could not traverse the streets of the city with a box askew—on the first turn you would lose it, most likely landing on a taxicab with two attorneys in the back seat.

Cooperation also meant the container sliding off the truck cleanly without sticking on its way down. Drivers didn't like to resort to tricks such as *the rev-it-up-to-4000-rpms-and-pop-the-clutch-technique* or another tried and true approach—*drive to the nearest overhead El track and nudge it off.*

Cooperation, of course, also meant agreeing to come up off the ground. This box was violating that rule; it apparently had been insulted or ignored, and was taking it out on me.

My morning had gone well up to this point, and I had made three uneventful trips to the transfer station. After I dropped my third box off in the yard, I was told that Cal DeJong, my mentor of old, was to go with me on the next journey. I was taken aback and a little irritated. Come on, I thought to myself, I know what I'm doing. Just give me the address; I can find the place.

We were quiet as Cal approached the cab. No verbalization. The fact that, at 280 + pounds, Cal could have twisted me into a pretzel had something to do with it. Besides, I did feel a slight sense of relief. I figured that Cal knew the city like his house and therefore the location of every one of the hundreds, if not thousands, of drop boxes the company had scattered around the city. And that could be nice, I thought, having my personal global positioning system riding next to me.

In truth, I often needed translation help. Typically, the company's radio dispatcher would garble some words and I would inevitably have to ask him to repeat it a couple of times. He wouldn't hide his frustration either, mumbling something about "stupid summer help." I would get pissed off at him for his inability to enunciate clearly, and our love affair would come to a rapid end.

"Nu#m*r 30, go to 12piτ59 N. Reωrφttδ St. and p϶♣k up the α∞yarder. See the μι for some import ∝t inf⊗ϖmatℵIn. Did yϕ get thτ?" would be a typical transmission.

Get that cigarette out of your mouth, I wanted to say, and speak into the mike. Yet apparently, the other drivers could understand the foreign tongue of "cityserviceradio" quite fluently. One dispatch of the directions and away they would go. What was wrong with me, I wondered?

For some reason today's dispatcher Dave was clearer than normal. Even as Cal was settling in to my passenger seat and I swore I felt my truck sag a little to the right, the speaker crackled with the directions. I learned that my destination was the intersection of State & Randolph, right in the heart of downtown Chicago, and that I was to pick up a 30-yarder. That's cool, I thought. I know right where to go.

The company I worked for had a long standing contract with one of the larger construction firms in the city. That company had snagged a multimillion dollar renovation contract with Marshall Field, and for the past several weeks had been demolishing the old North entrance to the State Street store. I had been there several times already. Seemed simple enough, I thought. So why Cal?

That was not all, Dave went on. The container was going to be full of girders, I-beams and other metal. Rather than bring the load back to the transfer station, I was to bring it to Chicago Steel & Iron for recycling. DeJong was coming with to show me the ropes.

I glanced at him. "So, Cal, I finally get to go to Chicago Steel & Iron today, huh? Not that I don't love your company, but why do I need you? Is it that hard to locate?"

"Na, it ain't hard to find." He began to chuckle to himself. "But it's one hell of a place to go through, that's for sure."

I looked at my watch, not liking that snicker of his. It was slightly after 11:45 AM. My destination was four miles away, at most. I figured we would arrive at State & Randolph a little after 12 noon—lunch hour in the city. The streets and sidewalks would be crawling with people, buses, taxis, cops, and cars the entire way.

A thought struck me. The trip could be something to which I could look forward. This was compensation for having to make a jaunt to the Loop in the daytime. The city center was where the beautiful people were, for sure. Smartly dressed women and classy businessmen would be strolling the sidewalks, networking, making gargantuan deals, and all that stuff. Yessiree. As I finagled my truck through the city streets I would gape at the throngs and wonder: that really tall guy—which college team is he on? Or I bet he's one of the Bulls on his way to an autographing session. And those three men smoking cigars and talking up a storm—I'll bet they're the heads of Sears, United Air Lines, and Standard Oil consummating a blockbuster of a merger. How about that stunning blonde with the $5,000 dress walking the stupid little poodle—didn't I see her on TV the other day? Is she who I think she is?

Why, I would then wonder, did I only see such beauty downtown? Since I was a truck driver I felt it incumbent for me to scrutinize all the women I passed, and I rarely encountered bombshells on the West Side, South Side, or the River North area. Was it just the outward trappings, their makeup, and wardrobe that made the Loop Ladies stunning? Or did the money, power, and job opportunities of Downtown act as a magnet for the beautifuls?

It wasn't only the sight of the gaga girls that made my Loop laps enjoyable. Being around the movers and shakers of the metropolis lent an air of importance to my mundane position, being a garbageman. At least in this part of town, I figured, it was important garbage, coming out of important buildings, made by important people.

Not like the place I was taking this load of mangled metal, I knew. I had heard of Chicago Steel & Iron before. In casual conversations in the drivers' lunchroom, the men would make nasty comments about the place, usually followed by some cussing or laughter. Chicago Steel was just not a location that you drove to, did what you were going for, and leave. The place had what they called *character.* But then, that seemed to be the case for most of the customers City Service had. Ah well, I thought, another learning curve to climb.

Cal let me find my way to the Marshall Field store without giving directions. Instead he rambled on about how he was hoping to someday move out of the city and buy some land in the country. I pictured him living out in some wide open expanse, walking through the corn fields and pastures, surrounded by livestock. I tried to picture that image. I really did. It just didn't click in my mind.

I've lost count of the guys I knew who fought the city all their lives, all the while verbalizing how one of these days they were moving out. From my observations ... it don't happen.

However, after he was done buying his 1,000 acres and stocking it with herds aplenty, Cal did spring a surprise on me. "Larry, soon as we arrive at Marshall's, I'm heading to the office of Walsh Construction and get tickets signed for all the loads that we picked up for them yesterday. Seemed there was some jackass running the show over at 453 Kedzie yesterday. He lost all the paperwork. So, you pick up the box, and I'll hoof it to their office at Lake and Wabash. You can pick me up on the way to Chicago Steel. I'll give ya 15-20 minutes. OK?"

"No problem. I'll see you at the corner," I said, with mixed feelings. I appreciated his trust in my ability to do this on my own, although I had a sense of unease at his leaving as well. It was now just me against the city. Cal's experience, if not he himself, was a nice companion.

Sure enough, once we crossed south over the Chicago River and passed under the rails of the Elevated, I could detect a different clientele on the streets. The dress of the pedestrians was smarter and they walked more quickly. After all, if you spend $10 million between your morning coffee and lunch, you probably have to move fast.

When we arrived at State & Randolph, and before I could even get down from the cab, a policeman blew his whistle, motioned for me to come on in with his left hand, and, with an authoritative look to his right hand, indicated to the noon rush that they must stop. Most obliged.

Here I come, important me. I winked at Mack, my dog companion on the hood of the truck. From out of nowhere a worker appeared and opened the temporary fenced gate. Little things like this made this job pleasurable. Forget the early mornings, the dust and debris that clung on my sweaty arms, the stench of the places I had to get into, and the tension from trying to maneuver my rig through the streets without hitting things. To have a cop stop traffic for me—that made some of aches and pains palatable.

I swung my truck around in preparation to backing in, and noted that the container was close to the gate's entrance. That meant that I wouldn't be able to back in completely, which further meant that my truck's cab would extend into the street.

OK, I can do this very public thing. Honking limousines and taxis, swerving delivery trucks, bike messengers by the score and hundreds of pedestrians walking behind, in front and around my truck as I attempt to do this will not—I repeat—will not rattle my cage.

I put my transmission in reverse and the beep-beep-beep warning began. In spite of the officer's best efforts, several cabs and a Mercedes Benz skirted behind my approach. His whistle seemed futile. I gamely continued to back up, knowing that as long as there was a margin of room, the flow of vehicles and pedestrians would continue.

Within seconds, my truck was crossing over the concrete sidewalk, forcing all but the most frantic of the crowd to pause. Yet, with my lumbering, dirty rig only a few feet from brushing against their $2000 Armani suits, two high-powered men of prestige and power walked foolishly on, only at the last moment quickening their step to avoid contact. A perfectly coifed brunette, armed with a smart handbag and two Nieman Marcus packages, did pause at the last second, giving me a look of annoyance and disgust.

I smiled. There was a sense of righteous anger rising inside me. To make these movers and shakers of the city take pause made my day. I applied the air brake with zest and the attendant *pshshshsh* of air seemed to startle some. I was here to do my job, let the others be damned.

Cal and I clambered out of our cab. He disappeared with the understanding that I was to pick him up at Walsh's office three blocks distant. I checked out the container. This looked to be a clean load, definitely no need for a tarp. Some of the usual piping, gnarled conduit, wiring and the like. I then noticed the large girders, half buried under the light stuff; steel beams that, for generations, had held up part of the north entrance. Unusual looking load, I thought. And heavy.

The operator of one of the Bobcats skittering back and forth and side to side stopped his machine when I approached to have him sign the ticket. "Hope she ain't too heavy, buddy," he noted with an ominous tone. "I warned the guys to go easy on this one."

"No problem," I bravely responded. I was confident in my truck's strength to pick this box up. I had a conventional cab with me today, with the engine in front. Its size made it harder to maneuver in traffic, but when it came to lifting heavy loads, this was the one to have. "If I had the cab-over from last week," I reassured him, "it might be a different story. Not to worry, there isn't a lot this baby can't pick up."

As I examined the load and repositioned some piping and loose wiring to keep them from landing on the street, second thoughts were creeping into my head. This sucker looks heavy, I thought, eyeing several girders. Wonder if my wheels will lift off the ground when I pick it up?

While most of the other disposal companies used trucks with gears, hooks and leverage bars, City Service trucks pulled the containers up by way of cables—big, strong, heavy, hunking cables. This system allowed for flexibility when working in narrow confines or where the height was limited; it also allowed a truck to literally turn a box sideways to pick it up or drop it off. But its weakness was evident when it was asked to pick up heavy—I mean really heavy loads. Sometimes it simply couldn't. Most often, however, we would succeed, but in the effort, the weight would cause the front end of the truck to lift off the ground a foot or two. A peculiar feeling came upon the driver as he would look out

his windshield and see the sky or tops of buildings rather than the street. Rumor was, that some drivers, when given the opportunity, would play "bouncy the trucky" just for the fun of it. But not me!

After getting the ticket signed, I cabled up and was ready to lift the box onto my truck's rails. I engaged the power takeoff, gave it some RPMs, and moved the lever. The truck tightened as it drew the container a few inches closer. It then stopped cold. "Yes, Mack," I informed my partner, "it is heavy." I gave it more RPMs. The cable moved another inch, and then halted. The container hadn't lifted off the ground even a bit. Feeling a little put out, my foot pushed down as far as it could on the pedal, the tachometer went to 5000 and the front of my truck began to work its way skyward. The box remained earthbound but my cab was now a few feet in the air. I backed off on the gas pedal and my cab returned to the ground. I heard mild expressions of wonderment from some of the pedestrians continually coursing by. I looked at the two Bobcat operators and they back at me. Their eyes said to try it again. I did, and this time floored it quickly, so as to kind of sneak up on it. My cab and I shot skyward again and the container rose perhaps one foot off the ground.

There I remained; smoke belching out of the exhaust stack and the engine approaching into the danger area in the tachometer. Meanwhile business men and women, throngs of shoppers and visitors stopped to take in the scene. I could see one youngster pull at his father's arm to draw his attention to this new tourist attraction.

After it became clear that my truck didn't have the intestinal fortitude to pick the load off the ground, I relaxed the pedal, the engine settled down and I came back to earth. This could not be done, I realized. I radioed the office and told Dave my predicament. He made an executive decision, rather hastily I thought, "You got to get it, dammit. I ain't got no other truck in the area, those guys are one of our better customers, and you better figure something out." His words of encouragement were reminiscent of Norman Vincent Peale.

I again crawled out of the truck, not so high and mighty this time. Some of the workers gathered around and offered up some suggestions. The Bobcat operator, who must have been the job foreman as well, barked some orders, and they began to rearrange some of the weight in the container, theorizing that with a different front to back weight ratio, I could get the box up and on the rails of the truck. As they reshuffled some puny portions of metal, I eyed the Bobcat itself and realized that it may have to help.

Within five minutes of furious exercises, we were ready to try it again. I followed the same procedures as before with only slightly better results. The box now rose three feet; still a little shy of the ledge I needed the box to clear. Again, my cab shot skyward and again, I became a source of amusement and wonder. By now the lunch hour crowd had gathered to be entertained.

The weather that day was very pleasant, and the streets were full. Office workers were able to munch on their bologna sandwiches and simultaneously ponder—Would the truck and its hapless driver win, or would the heavyweight champion of all containers remain steadfast on the ground, and the man go home in ignominious defeat?

The crowds could very well have been betting on the outcome. By now, I was embarrassed as well as nervous. I had to pick this thing up and be on my way. My dispatcher had sent me—summer help—to do this veteran-like thing. If I would disappoint him, I would most likely only receive scrub assignments from then on.

I approached the Bobcat driver who seemed to be the boss. Would he be willing to maneuver the bucket of his mini-bulldozer under one side of the box once my truck had raised it up three feet, and then help lift? In fact, could both operators, one on each side, place their buckets underneath? I realized that I was asking a lot of them. If the cable was to break or the truck somehow lose its power, the tremendous weight of the container would come down and the two operators would be jackknifed into the side and seriously hurt.

To my surprise and relief, they both assented. They knew that as long as that box remained there, no empty was coming to take its place. No empty, no place to put the construction debris. No work getting done and that was unacceptable. Besides, I think it seemed a challenge to them, and though I could detect a little concern from one, we agreed. To help, I had even decided that I would put it in reverse and try to literally drive the truck under the box.

It had now been 15 minutes since I arrived and Cal was probably standing on the corner of Lake and Wabash. Amidst all the commotion, the truck radio informed me that Dave had already ordered Unit 22 to bring his empty box to State and Randolph. The other driver might be here any minute. It was now or never, and I knew that *never* was not in the vocabulary of City Services & Recycling.

I pulled myself up into the cab, and the Bobcats and their captains skittered to their positions on either side of the box. This was to be an assault from three fronts, and if I had had the use of another machine, I would have sent to him to attack the rear. This was war!

As I turned around in my cab to view the scene through the back window, I mentally went through the proper procedure, wanting to get this right …

'Step one'—let off the air brake. Jeez ... look at all the people walking around me, behind me, in front of me. Wish I was in some remote alley or parking lot. Get out of the way, folks!

'Step two'—put the power takeoff in gear. I've been here way too long. Should have been gone by now. Cal is probably wondering where the heck I am.

'Step three'—verify that my rear end is aligned fairly straight. It is ... straight enough ... I think. That cable better not snap at a time like this ... nah, none ever has. Then why do I think of it happening, with the broken end whipping through the cab, slicing it in half like a loaf of bread? Why? Because of those stories that some of the guys tell over lunch, that's why!

'Step four'—put the clutch in and slip the truck in lowest reverse. These folks are going to get a show. Any TV cameras around? The Bobcat guys seem a little nervous as well.

'Step five'—using both hands, grab the hoist and cable levers. I guess I don't need to steer this thing. The guys at the garage never showed me how to do this, but last summer Cal said it was one of the tricks that some used. Well, I don't like doing tricks, not here, not in the Loop at noon.

'Step six'—bring up the RPMs. So, because this box is so gol-dang heavy, I'm gonna try to drive my truck under it? Yep!

'Step seven'—pop the clutch and hope it works. *Help!*

The cacophony and hustle and bustle of the street were interrupted by the synchronized roars of the two Bobcats and my Cummins diesel at top power. The cable turned taut and the box began its inexorable slow climb against my truck's back plate as people stopped to stare. By now, my cab had risen to heights unimagined; the heavy tires a full four feet off the ground. My partners on their machines were giving it their full throttle as well, and the container continued its movement, inch by inch, until only a sliver of steel remained as a wall between the rails and the bottom of the box, between failure and success. Out of the corner of my eye, I could see the masses gawking at the struggle of the century. I could hear shouts of "*yea,*" "*go,*" and "*push.*"

Suddenly, as with a final surge, the truck and Bobcat trio, assisted emotionally by the throngs on the sidewalk, pulled and pushed the bottom ledge of the container up and over the wall. The box proceeded to slide up the rails the way it was intended and, within seconds, with equilibrium restored, my cab began to return from its voyage to outer space.

I breathed a sigh of relief, and to my surprise, heard shouts of "atta boy" and some light applause from the crowd. The noonday shoppers, business leaders, and tourists had become spectators in a new sport. Flush with the exhilaration of victory, I pulled out of Marshall Fields and wended my way up Wabash Avenue to Lake Street to meet up with Cal, tour guide for my next venture.

15

Chicago Steel & Iron

Flush with the experience at Marshall Fields, I arrived at Lake and Wabash, finding Cal DeJong waiting for me as planned. We worked our way north to Ontario Street, to get onto the Kennedy Expressway and to head to Chicago Steel & Iron. Passing by Hard Rock Café, the Fifties McDonalds, Ed Debevics, and the slew of other hot spots on the near North Side was of mild interest to me by now, but I knew that visitors from far and near didn't think so. Here was the part of town where tourists and teenyboppers hung out, and a wealth of fun and play was evident in the architecture along the stretch and the snazzy cars cruising the road—a different venue altogether from the Loop.

We hit all the green lights, and within moments we were on I-94 heading to the industrial region up north along the Chicago River. When I exited ten minutes later, the geography had changed drastically. This was an area of medium to heavy manufacturing, a part of the city that showed its dirty teeth and hearty laugh. The sounds of train engines churning, boxcars coupling, presses stamping, and people producing were all around me. There was also an odor pervading the air that I could not quite pin down; however, one thing was clear—it was the smell of work.

Cal guided me through a series of lefts and rights till we arrived at Clybourn to head north yet a little more. He indicated a final left turn; I obliged, and was surprised to find myself on a short, crowded street. My view was limited to a distance of less than a block, yet that stretch was bumper to bumper trucks.

Cal indicated that we had arrived and that I was to get in line. "The place is just ahead. This won't take but just a few minutes."

Sure enough, within seconds the rig ahead, another container truck like mine, moved up a length and I followed. Almost immediately I noticed that another truck had pulled in behind me. This line seemed to move slowly, steadily, yet was always filled. Though my vision ahead was obscured, I could see scores of people milling about the street. Within several minutes the trucks ahead of me had pulled away and I arrived at the intersection. There a panorama laid spread out before me. I looked to the south; for two full city blocks there snaked a line of dilapidated pickups, station wagons, and assorted small vehicles, overflowing with scrap metal of all types. In each vehicle sat two, three or more individuals, trying to pass the time as best they could.

I glanced to my right and could make out tractor-trailers streaming from the north. A pattern was set. The little people, the scavengers eking out a living, were assigned to the southern approach; the container trucks were to line up from the east and the semis from the north.

However, my eyes were most drawn to what lay directly before me—Chicago Steel and Iron, the goal of scrap-carrying vehicles from all over the northwest side. This was a feast for the senses, a sea of men, machinery, and ubiquitous activity.

Like a giant hurricane with numerous appendages flowing in and out, the eye of the storm was a half acre of twisted, mangled metal. From the north, south, east, and west we came to divulge our prizes gleaned from daily hunts throughout the city. And sitting like a monstrous queen ant astride her nest, engulfed to her armpits in metal offerings, ensconced in the shards of civilization, was a gigantic pincer-like machine. While rotating on a 180° line, it was being fed a steady diet of steel, iron and other metals by two always-moving, always-pushing, always-grabbing loaders. This pincer's sole mission was to grab, cut and feed; grab, cut and feed.

The object of its nourishment was a gargantuan conveyor belt that in turn fed an even larger machine with the apt name of Pulverizer. Into this steel-eating processor poured a steady diet of the remains of car bodies, stoves, radiators, refrigerators, beams, and every size and shape of metal imaginable. On the west side of this monolithic building, astride the Chicago River, were two additional belts, under which were positioned a like number of tractor-trailers being fed fine steel screenings or non-metallic detritus that the Pulverizer could not digest. This constant feeding and spewing forth of material struck me as the obscene bowel movements of a metal-eating monster.

The odor that pervaded this neighborhood was that of burning iron, coming from men with acetylene torches crawling over mounds of rubble, carving out valuable metals from appliances, automobiles and other objects that had given up the ghost years ago.

Though the sights and smells were fascinating, the sounds that belched forth from this storm of activity were even more surreal. The reverberation of the traffic on the elevated Kennedy one half-mile west played a background hum to the scores of vehicles lined up to pay homage. A loudspeaker emanating from somewhere was shrilling out commands, and whistles were blowing. The constant grindings of the Pulverizer and its belts, the groaning of the rotating pincer-like creature that fed it, and the loaders feeding the pincer combined to make a horrific noise. If hell has a sound, this was it.

"Quite the sight, ain't it," said Cal. "This place never ceases to amaze me." He paused for a second, and then pointed straight ahead. "Watch that guy there, with the straw hat. He's the one you got to keep your eye on. Get on the wrong side of him and it'll cost you five minutes or more every time you come here."

Situated in the middle of the intersection was a ruffled, simply dressed individual, with a swarthy complexion, a jutting nose, and a flat mouth that neither went up or down. The only remarkable feature about him was his wide-brimmed Panama. He evidently was traffic coordinator of this spaghetti junction. He determined which of the container trucks, semis, or scavengers could inch forward. And after every vehicle had weighed in on the scale, it was the straw hat who determined where and when you were to dump your precious load. It was evident that this world of chaos was his domain.

Every truck had to enter the yard and circumnavigate the Pulverizer on its way to the scale. After the weight was recorded and the truck had dumped, it was another trip around the yard to weigh empty. Airports and railroad switching yards are no better organized.

The man in the straw hat motioned to one of the scrap metal scavengers in a twenty-year-old van seemingly held together by baling wire and he, with his wife and two kids in tow, was allowed to proceed. The snake of humanity in tired-out pickups, station wagons, vans, and trailers moved forward another fifteen feet. There had to be seventy or more of them coming from the south, and my feelings of sympathy were mixed with my concern that I had to wait for all of them. Just when I began to think that my turn wouldn't come for ages, to my surprise, the straw hat looked me in the eye and pointed his finger.

"That's your cue, Larry." Cal advised. "Go now or wait another five."

"How come I got to go so quickly?" I asked, as I rapidly shifted through three gears. "I just got here! Some of those small guys probably been waiting for a half-hour."

"Even longer, I imagine. We're special, that's why. Our company gives 'em good business. They know Mr. Monsma isn't going to send our trucks to sit and wait for hours. This ain't the only scrap yard in town, just the biggest."

As I cautiously went through several gears, I began to realize that I'd been given preferential treatment two times today, yet this seemed even more special.

I made the wide circuitous route around the recycling yard and got an eyeful. From every angle I saw industrial filth, heard fearsome sounds, and smelled odorous fumes. This was an apocalyptic scene for any environmentalist who would have stumbled upon this place, though I doubted that any would venture into this neighborhood.

I drove up onto the scale and stopped, pausing for a few seconds, when a slight panic set in. "Cal, now what do I do? How can I tell when they got my weight? If they are yelling at me to go, I can't hear anything, it's so noisy around this place. Am I supposed to go in to the office or...?"

Before Cal, with a serene smile on his face, could even say a word, a shrill blast from a horn broke into the din. There was no mistaking the intent of that signal. I lurched off the scale without hesitation. "Now just work your way out into the street," instructed my relaxed partner, "and get ready to back in."

I began my laborious turning in a wide circle, preparing myself for what was sure to be a harrowing ordeal of backing my way through the throng of vehicles. Cal noted my concern and reassured me. "Don't worry, Lar. The straw hat's got everything under control."

A glance in my mirrors told me Cal was right. The hat was waving at me with one hand and pointing with the other to the direction I was to go. To my surprise, every other truck and man politely waited. No horns. No dirty looks from the semi drivers, no vile imprecations from the scavenger family next in

line in the ancient Suburban with their treasures flowing out the side and back windows. No cutting in front or behind, like the battle I had gone through at State and Randolph. The straw hat man was master of his universe, this intersection near Clybourn and the River North.

Putting my faith in his directions and not concerning myself with the vehicles and workers wandering about, I reversed my rig with ease. As I passed the man in the straw hat and nodded to him, I noticed he took a good look at me, no doubt putting my features in his memory banks for future reference. This guy was good.

My load, as heavy as it was, slid out with a satisfying din, literally pushing the truck forward as it poured out. The rest of the routine went as could be expected. I retraced my route around the yard to reweigh empty. After the horn's blast again startled me off the scale, I pulled the truck across the intersection where the hat man was still keeping order. Cal indicated that it was up to me to get the ticket signed.

The building that was the headquarters of all this bee-like activity was an ancient, ramshackle affair, giving the appearance that it had been on the river to greet LaSalle in the 1600s. The wooden steps leading up to the office on the second floor were worn bare in the middle, with a half-inch thick coat of residue lying on the edges. Placards in Spanish and English were plastered on the walls and doors. I hustled up the landing and found myself in a dirty-floored office, with four desks hiding behind a dingy, gray counter. The hum of air ventilation filled the room. The telephones were ringing, and an occasional loudspeaker message carried on with the atmosphere outside. There was a line for tickets to pay and money to give.

Off in a corner, seemingly oblivious to the racket, appeared to be Mr. Chicago Steel himself. He was a smallish man, in his fifties, with pure white hair and puffy cheeks. Standing by a window, and smoking an oversize stogie, he was watching the metal and the money come in. Suddenly turning to me and noting that I was the driver of the big blue rig that had dumped the load of girders and beams, he quietly said, "Nice load, son."

An awkward "Thanks" was all I could utter.

I signed the frail little slip of paper the secretary thrust my way, slipped the copy she gave me in my pocket, and scurried down the steps. Back in the cab, Cal, my ever-present companion Mack, and I wended our way back to City Disposal's garage. As I passed the hordes of down and outers in their beaten old cars and trucks, I saw poverty, meekness, politeness, and fatigue in each face. The women wore no jewelry or makeup; their children displayed old castoff clothing. No beauty, no fancy trappings, no pretentiousness, no power, no prestige here. It seemed to me that these people would remain in line and in poverty for time interminable. Twenty years later, they are probably still there.

16

One Man's Trash ...

Spring 1992

The call came late on Monday afternoon—they wanted the work to begin the next day, just after regular closing hours. Our bosses, and to some extent, we, the drivers, were expecting it. "It" was a special job of cleanup for one of our bigger customers. The manpower requested and the effort to be expended put this rubbish pickup on a gargantuan scale, and although we had an inkling of what might be found, the reality of what we began to toss into the trash heap was startling, even to guys used to seeing wealth turned into waste.

* * *

On April 13, 1992, the "City of the Big Shoulders" was having problems unlike any other. Leave it to Chicago, the metropolis that turned its river around to flow backwards, to also have that same river spring a leak. The Chicago River, a meandering waterway that had, over the years, served as highway, dividing line between neighborhoods, and garbage dump was exacting its revenge on the urban mess that had grown around it.

In the early 1900s engineers devised and built a series of tunnels in the central part of the city that connected many of the bigger buildings. These subterranean highways had tracks upon which small railcars at one time carried coal, refuse, and other necessities of commerce. The tunnels were forty to sixty feet below the city surface in some sections, and connected the third and fourth basement levels of several downtown buildings. For years, the passageways made sense, but in time, the size limitation of the underground cars, combined with improved transportation appearing on the city's streets, convinced many merchants and property managers to forget the warrens they had built. Yet they remained down there for many decades—as many as forty miles of subterranean passageways—unused and forgotten, classic examples of 'out of sight and out of mind.' By the 1990s only a relatively few maintenance people and building engineers knew of their existence.

That is, until the Great Lakes Dredge and Dock Company was hired to replace old pilings near the Kinzie Street bridge crossing the river. Drilling into what they had expected to be solid rock, or at least Chicago River muck, the men unknowingly tapped into the roof of one section of tunnel. Over the next several months, something remarkable and unseen by any human eye was occurring. A tiny crack grew and a trickle of river water began to increase in volume. Finally, on the morning of April 13, the river developed a full blown hole in that portion of the tunnel. Unfortunately, many sections of the almost one hundred year old network were still connected and the recipe for an urban disaster was complete. To officials racing to the scene overlooking the river, it appeared that the Chicago River and everything in it would be sucked into a toilet-like whirlpool, not unlike what one sees on ancient explorer maps.

Of course, the water had to go somewhere. Quickly the tunnels became torrents of a murky liquid rushing from basement to basement. Soon the storerooms of some of the major retailers in the Loop began to take on the appearance of Mississippi River towns during a Midwest spring, with even a few fish swimming amidst the fine furnishings and clothes. The city took most of a day to plug its leak and many more days for the vile liquid to be pumped out and the stores to reopen.

That had been a few weeks ago, and now rumors were spreading that deep in the basements of some of the city's finest stores there lay millions of dollars worth of spoiled merchandise. Then our company received the call. We were to report to work for the next several days at staggered times, working extended shifts and running the operation around the clock. This was partially to alleviate the jam of midday traffic and, to some extent, to keep the news of what was occurring as low key and out of sight as possible.

* * *

Something rather unflattering develops in the human psyche when mass amounts of money, goods, or food become suddenly available. The looting mentality almost kicked in among the drivers as truck after truck backed in to the docks of the downtown stores, and the retailers disgorged their soggy basements of ruined, halfway ruined or only slightly ruined material. "What can I get?" became the mantra on everybody's lips.

Of course, that example of "wealth turning to waste" is not the only occurrence that those in the scavenger business have observed. Every garbio has seen it occasionally and those who haul from the city's factories and merchandisers see it often. From the 1950s on, with assembly line efficiency and large warehousing abilities, production line mistakes and missed deadlines created large volumes of waste. Restaurants toss out huge amounts of food, well-to-do residents of the city and suburbs routinely rid themselves of their riches, and construction crews dispose of building materials that could, with a little effort, be recycled.

It was natural that trash haulers became, in a way, society's first environmentalists. Most residents of the city and suburbs would not take the effort to gather their few samples of valuables, nor would it pay for them to bring the materials to distant recycling centers. Long before it became the province of mainstream America, scavengers realized that collecting bits of brass, aluminum, and copper over many weeks and months will, in time, produce large volumes.

Yet, the epitomes of urban environmentalists are the transients and bottom dwellers of the city, eking out a living by gathering metals, batteries, paper, pallets, and other fruits of the urban jungle. They, in effect, are the experts in urban survival. Their efficiency is at once marvelous and pitiful to witness. Many a homeless man or woman, as well, will find their supper in the dumpsters of supermarkets, the next day's earnings from scavenged wire, and furniture from cardboard boxes and wooden skids. Some go too far in their scavenging, stripping copper wire from light poles and walking off with manhole covers, but that is another story.

When I worked on the garbage truck, my guilt feelings failed to kick in after finding some item of value. Rather, there was always a sense of serendipity and even frugality in retrieving an object from the landfill. The description of what I could find was without limit.

Since I smoked cigarettes for many years, I understood the value of always having a lighter in my possession. The number of cigarette lighters that residents of the North Side suburbs disposed rather flippantly in their trash was astounding. The majority would invariably work if I simply put in a flint or refilled the fluid.

The idea of multiple speakers for a sound system was in vogue in the 1970s and I made it my goal to collect every one I could retrieve. Within half a summer of labor, I amassed twelve speakers of various sizes, scavenging from old television sets, radios and record players. My parents' basement had wall to wall to wall to wall woofers, with a few ceiling tweeters thrown in for good measure.

While I was in college, my pocketbook was limited, but my imagination on what I could do with new-found goodies was not. I furnished my dorm room with the flotsam and jetsam of Chicagoland. Nifty looking wine and whiskey bottles, cool paintings still in their cheap frames, and slightly used desk lamps were favorite items to salvage from the landfill's grasp. All of these went well with my room décor—*Early American Landfill.* On occasion old tables, chairs, and even carpet were kept from the jaws of the hungry packer truck and strapped temporarily to the side or top of my rig until I could get back to base. If there was no room to put it on the truck, I would take note of the address and be back within a few hours on my way home. I needed to be creative to haul a 12 by 20 foot carpet on a ten-year-old Toyota down the Eisenhower, but I learned that it could be done.

Not all things salvaged were a wise choice. I once made the mistake of taking home a rather large plush teddy bear found sitting next to the garbage can, cute as ever and in excellent shape! This was a great find for my four kids, I thought, no doubt about it. It wasn't until a week later, when our carpet was hopping with fleas, that I realized the motivation of the original owner. The next day the flea farm was at the curb waiting for *my* garbageman to pick up. Who knows—that same stuffed animal may yet be making the rounds of the area.

Occasionally we would find items that individuals have tossed by mistake. For what reason would someone dump a perfectly good pair of work boots, barely used? Or that working flashlight, the crescent wrench, the watch that still gave the correct time, and the thermos bottle filled with coffee?

Some objects led me to realize there were interesting stories behind the mysterious disposals. Certain types of clothing in "like new" condition and photographs still in the picture frames gave indications of heartbreaks, and arguments, deaths, and divorce. One colleague was called on to bring hundreds of cases of dated beer to the landfill, accompanied by a company representative to verify the dirty deed was actually done. I found twenty bowling balls one time that had four holes mistakenly drilled in them. Did an employee get canned for that foul-up?

As I worked the streets of the metropolitan area, I often wished I could have a wagon trailing behind my truck to collect the riches and wonders of America's trash. Often, however, the shear volume of the find was overwhelming. When a cold storage facility realized that an entire shipment of vegetables was one day past due, our truck was given the dubious honor of disposing of the daily minimum requirements for a thousand people. And when a cargo of well-known chocolate candy bars was unloaded right before my eyes in the landfill, I was reminded of the expression "enough to feed an army." The one case of chocolate I wrestled into my cab kept my family in pimples for months.

Thinking about what other garbagemen had found over the years encouraged me to again seek out my friends in the Holland Home for the Elderly after not seeing them for a year. If I had discovered great serendipity in my limited experiences, I could only imagine what they had seen themselves or the great finds they had heard of from the 'old boy network.' Convinced that these trash haulers were walking treasures of information (I recalled that only two were now walking), I made an appointment. Besides, I realized, it was high time I did some visiting. I had heard that Cal Pettinga had passed away and that John Van Otten had had some health issues, and I was eager to see how the others were doing.

I located them in the outdoor patio overlooking the west driveway. The four elderly men were sitting in a straight line, Teunis Riemersma and Paul DeGraaf comfortably resting in chaise lounges and Jake Ouwinga in his wheelchair. I was surprised to see that John Van Otten was also consigned to a wheelchair and I could perceive rather quickly that he had aged considerably since I had last seen him. His eyes seemed to not focus well on whoever was speaking, and the few words that he uttered were feeble indeed.

This place was their favorite spot, one of the attendants informed me, and every day, weather permitting, they maneuvered themselves there. The sun kept them toasty warm, the three walls surrounding the walkway blocking any cool fall breeze. The men had a vantage point overlooking the sidewalk about 80 feet away, framed by a Kelly-green lawn in immaculate condition. Thirty feet beyond the walkway was the road. The sidewalk, with its occasional pedestrian, and the street, always an excellent source of eye food, provided plenty of people to observe and comment on.

This was Thursday, and every fourth day of the week meant the coming and going of the garbage truck. Actually, in the short time I was there, we saw three trucks pass our way. In addition to the regular rear-loading packer, we observed the latest technology in recycling—a four-compartment vehicle, with its bins accessible from either side. A third rig, a packer designated for grass and leaves, was also in use. It was more evidence that specialization had come to the trash-hauling industry.

The five of us intently watched the movements of the young men as they nimbly leaped out of their cabs, moving in fluid movements to the back or the side to do their labors. The garbage and recycling trucks seemed to work in a pattern of sorts, running the same block, only on opposite sides. Fifteen minutes later the grass truck appeared.

Riemersma was the first to give his opinion that morning. "I bet teir boss won't like to see tem working tese blocks togeter like tat. If we see te company pickup come by, I bet you tat he separates tem."

"Why's that?" I asked.

DeGraaf chimed in, "Cause the man's afraid his guys is going to sit around and gab, not keep working. Ya know how bosses dink. Dey dink dat da guys will stop da trucks every once in awhile, yuck it up and cause a traffic jam on da side street. He thinks it don't look good, and dat da customers are gonna complain. And dat's too bad, too, cause I 'member it was fun to work togeder ... just to see da other guys reminds you you're on a team." His visage turned a dour gray as perhaps old and long gone coworkers came to mind. "I always liked it."

Riemersma and Van Otten agreed with a nod of their heads, with the Dutchman adding his characteristic spit onto the grass. I could tell Jake Ouwinga, always looking at it from the owner's point of view, was going to add his thoughts. I wasn't disappointed.

"Well, it's easy for you men to talk," Ouwinga sermonized, "but you never received calls from the ladies who felt intimidated by three or four rough-looking and rough-sounding guys 'yucking it up,' as you put it, in front of their driveway."

"Why dose ladies," interjected DeGraaf, with a grin spreading across his face and a mock look of concern, "what's so bad about some guys wit sweat pouring down deir bare backs, wid grimy boots, and grimier still gloves having a beer on da street in front of your house?"

Riemersma and DeGraaf winked at each other. Van Otten muttered something unintelligible, but I think he was off in another world by this point in the conversation.

"Well, precisely my point, DeGraaf." Ouwinga retorted, almost cracking a smile himself. "We garbios were always appreciated for what we did, as long as it was at a distance."

"Mr. Ouwinga," I was direct and to the point this morning, "Did you ever let your men scavenge through the garbage? You know, keep aluminum, copper, brass and other stuff they could find?"

DeGraaf and Riemersma turned to their partner. I thought I could detect Van Otten raising his eyes a little.

I went on. "The reason I ask is, from what I've heard, the owners have stopped all that nowadays. If they catch you scrapping—one warning ... the second time—you're gone."

"Well, we did ... sometimes." Ouwinga paused. "Mind you, it was hard to stop it altogether. At one point we told the men they had to store their keepsakes outside the garage. I know that idea went over like a lead balloon."

"Make a mess," was the surprising and not entirely coherent opener from Van Otten, who up to this point had not uttered a word. The four of us glanced at him as if looking for more. He muttered something low and incomprehensible, but drew quiet once more.

Ouwinga felt he needed to explain. "What John means is that often the drivers would take a good thing and make a mess of it. It wasn't just the bosses who became irritated with the pack rats; the insurance companies would get on our case to clean things up around the garage, sometimes even the health department, if you can imagine that. "

DeGraaf offered his view. "Man, Jake. I remember your place down on Laramie. You guys used to have barrels along da side of da garage wall just to collect da brass, wire, batteries and all dat stuff. That was good, good for dem and good for you, wasn't it? Less to dump."

Ouwinga nodded and was uncharacteristically quiet.

DeGraaf went on. "I know some of da garages allowed scrapping if a percentage went to da owners. And dat was OK. We all did scavenging." He went on, looking at me square in the eye, and now a little agitated. "You worked on da truck years ago, in da good times, young fella. You could scrap. It's changed now; ain't like it used to be."

DeGraaf's face suddenly lit up. "Old Doug Feller, you guys remember him?" Riemersma and Ouwinga nodded, while Van Otten said something vaguely referring to the flower pot to his right.

DeGraaf continued, with a smile. "He was good, had an eye for dat stuff. He used to save up so much all year long, dat he could buy all his Christmas presents dat way. He kept a separate account just from da money he would scrounge up."

The usual rejoinder came from Ouwinga. "Well, yes, Paul, but it was because of some of those guys that we had to quit. They'd ruin it. They'd always leave a mess around the place, sometimes stealing from the others .... Or maybe claiming something was took. I don't know. I do know that some fights started over who was keeping scrap, and where they were stashing it."

Riemersma now added to the conversation, "Well, we neber had any troubles at our place, Jake. And tat is ta truth. In fact, since we had a lot of young guys—summer help (he looked at me and winked)—it was only me and Bob Elzinga tat kept scrap piles. We done pretty good too, I might add.

"But te kids, tey didn't know how to look for stuff either. We older guys knew where te riches lay hidden." He again looked at me. "Young man, did you know tat te hub caps of some of te older cars were brass, just covered over with chrome? Brass too good to dump in te truck, I'll tell you."

"So you kept old hub cabs too?" I was incredulous, "And bring them in for money?"

"Not every one. I couldn't keep 'em all, cause I would find one everyday, it seems. And just te brass ones."

"How could you tell?" I asked. I pictured myself standing on the street with a hub cap in hand, examining it from all angles, and wondering if it was a keeper.

"Hey man," DeGraaf chimed in, smile across his face like he knew a trade secret, "a simple scratch on da pavement would show ya if it was good or not. Of course, when folks tossed old toilets, faucets, and sinks, dose also were a good source of copper and brass."

I grimaced; mentally kicking myself for all the old plumbing fixtures I had thrown out.

DeGraaf, seeing the look on my face, continued, "Course, no one never threw out car batteries; dey were a buck apiece for a while."

More grimacing.

Riemersma, who worked residential more than the others, had another source. "Yah, te batteries vas good. Some furniture good too, I tell ya. I remember every time we found stuffed sofas, we crunched 'em up in te truck, and ten we often got rewards. We'd find coins aplenty falling on te street, or lying in te bottom of te hopper after it cycled. I kind of felt we was panning for gold."

Ouwinga, true to form, put it in perspective. "Well, looking back, I think the 1950s to 1970s were the best years for scrapping. Everything's become more plastic, less copper and brass; and more is recycled before it gets to the curb or loading dock. And the big companies think that workers work better if they're not diving into the garbage looking for goodies." He turned reflective a moment, no doubt thinking of the men and machines he oversaw for years. "At least that's what my nephew tells me, the one who still works for Waste. I suppose they're right."

"Should recycle us ...." came the surprise declaration from Van Otten, and the others winced when he said it. I glanced at the old gentleman in the wheelchair, eyes half closed, staring off into space. He suddenly fired off another shocker. "We're ready for the trash heap, like old rags ...." and then he closed his eyes tight and retreated into quiet.

"Do you miss running your place, Mr. Ouwinga?" I suddenly blurted. I have no idea why those words came out, but out they did. I turned to the others. "Do you men miss the streets, the work, the other guys?"

There was silence for a time. DeGraaf eventually responded, showing clarity and wisdom from a source I hadn't expected. "Friend, since we left da business, it's gone off on its own. It done left us like we used ta leave old sawdust on da garage floor."

Ouwinga's eyes were fixed on DeGraaf as he spoke, while Riemersma was squinting at me. Van Otten appeared to be miles or years away, but could have been listening for all I knew. DeGraaf went on, "You guys talk about recycling stuff ... well, we're gonna be recycled too someday, like old metal or paper."

As the others remained silent, apparently listening with interest, DeGraaf sensed encouragement and continued, "We just sit here now, waiting for da Time to come, and dat's fine. We had our heyday. I imagine you did too, young fella. The younger ones is having 'em now, and den some day dey will be here too ... here, or some other place." He paused and turned to the table on his right for a glass of water that wasn't there. I tried to get the attention of the attendant but failed. "I ain't bitter. Don't get me wrong. I had a good life. You guys all say da same?" he questioned.

Riemersma nodded. "Good words, friend." He closed his eyes.

Ouwinga, his eyes steeled to the thoughts, remained silent. Van Otten too was mum, his eyelids shut. This seemed a spiritual moment for the five of us. Brief, but like a window to their lives that opened for a second and closed again. It was enough. I suddenly felt like I was intruding in their space. I knew it was time for me to go.

* * *

I said my good-byes to the four and found my way out. Noting the time, I realized that I had not eaten lunch yet. Near North Avenue and Route 83, I knew, was a bakery that offered some of the better croissant sandwiches in the suburbs. It was too much to resist the clarion call, and though it was out of my way, I rationalized, it was definitely worth the trip.

Six minutes later I was faced with the difficult decision between a chocolate cream croissant or a ham and Swiss. Not wanting to offend either, three minutes later I walked out with both. As I retired to the privacy of my car to listen to the Cubs play the Giants while I relished my lunch, I witnessed an interesting affair in human foibles.

A homeless man, a rarity in this community, had been investigating the bakery's dumpster for choice leftovers. While I munched on my pastry, a policeman arrived on the scene to catch the man in the 'dastardly act'. With discreteness the officer gave a vocal reprimand to the man that he not be seen there again. This was enough to send the poor fellow skulking away.

I realized I was again witnessing the loss of valued goods. This time it was not high fashion clothes from a large Chicago retailer, copper wire salvaged from a construction site, or even recyclable cardboard that was being wasted. This was the most basic—food—and it too would soon be tossed into a truck and sent to some great hill miles beyond.

I continued to feed my face with the soft and delicate bread even as the transient disappeared down the street, while the officer reported in on his radio. Life, as I recalled learning from a certain U. S. president, was indeed unfair.

My mind was distracted to the more important affairs at hand. Sandberg had just hit a homer in the eighth and the Cubbies were now ahead. I remained there for a while, enjoying the last morsels of my meal and the resurgent Northsiders.

Soon the victory was complete and, with a smile in my heart, realized it was time to get home. As I drove along Spring Road, I observed it was garbage pickup day here as well. I hadn't gone a mile when I came upon the same patrol car that had intercepted the man at the bakery. The policeman was out at the side of the curb examining what appeared to be numerous paint cans resting next to some garbage containers. Draped over the cans was a hand-drawn sign that read, *Free Paint—old, but still good.* Quite possibly recalling that his house needed refreshing, the officer scooped up four of the gallons and placed them gingerly in the trunk of his squad car, hopped back in and drove off.

17

Cold Memories

1995

The snow glistened, shimmering and sparkling clean, unusual for the city, as I exited the house and made for my car. Several inches of new-fallen ice crystals blanketed the old, and left a beautiful topping to enjoy for a short time. Soon, I knew, it would melt, or more likely, become coated with a thin veneer of city air. Emerging from the shade of the garage, I mildly cursed myself for not remembering my sunglasses, for the glare of the sun off the carpet of white fluff was blinding. However, it being months since the sun last had any intensity, I wouldn't have had a clue as to where my shades were. And it seemed an affront to complain about anything so bright and pure, so I gamely continued, squinting in pain down the streets of the western suburbs. My destination was only five miles distant, I reassured myself. I would switch eyeballs every other block.

It was indeed cold, I realized, as my car's heater struggled to produce some warmth. The stillness and dryness of the air belied the fact that the temperature, now reported on the car's radio, hovered at -15°, making this the kind of chill that can sneak up on a person who may be outside for any length of time.

Thankful that my car was soon beginning to pump out some semblance of BTU's, and that no gas line freeze had caused it to stall, I turned onto Meyers Avenue. Noting that this must be "garbage day," a shiver of understanding crept into my frosty fingers as I observed the many cans half buried in snowplow hills that the garbagemen would have to kick and pull to empty that morning. Fighting the elements was part and parcel of the job, but bone-chilling days like this ranked at the bottom. Refuse frozen in the cans and containers encased in ice made work in these conditions particularly brutal. Unless one was well protected, frostbite or at the least, numb toes and hands would develop within an hour. I put the heater up a notch.

By the time I arrived at the Holland Home for the Elderly after an absence of several months, the radiator had finally accomplished its objective in sending some welcomed warmth. I turned the motor off and thought I could hear the manifold growl back at me. Now that the engine had gotten to its efficiency, it was thinking, the owner didn't want it on anymore and turned the key … go figure.

Realizing that I was thinking about my engine thinking, I thought to myself, *I'm going to wind up in this home sooner than I want to.* Scratching my head and wondering which room they would put me in, I headed for the Cicero lounge to find my elderly friends.

I spotted Jake Ouwinga in the corner by the Reader's Digest bookcase, in his wheelchair, nodding off in the land of half-consciousness. He had what appeared to be a Bible in his lap, with his ever-present thick lens glasses resting on top. Teunis Riemersma was in front of the television with a few others—the show being one of the nature stories the attendants always considered safe and non-controversial. The volume was turned so low, however, that it was doubtful any of the residents could make out what was being described. Perhaps the attendants considered the action on the screen sufficient.

Neither Paul DeGraaf nor John Van Otten were there, and since I had always had pleasant conversations with the four in the past, I thought it proper to ask one of the staff if it was OK for me to bring the two gentlemen in so the five of us could have a visit.

"I'll check on Mr. DeGraaf; he may be able to come," Margie, the attendant on duty, hesitated. "Hadn't you heard? Mr. Van Otten suffered another stroke two days ago and is in the hospital. The family's been with him quite a bit; they don't think he's going to last long." She sighed, "And he's only seventy years."

"No, I hadn't heard …." I began, but Margie was already on her way to DeGraaf's room. "Surprised, and yet not so," I thought to myself. The last time I visited he had been looking feeble. I recalled that summer many years ago when Van Otten had hired me to work on the truck. The words of some hymn I hadn't sung in a long time came back, how *Time, like an ever-rolling stream, bears all its sons away; we fly forgotten, as a dream dies at the opening day.* John Van Otten was soon to be borne away.

I sat down next to Mr. Ouwinga—I thought it appropriate, suddenly, to think of him as Mister—and gently woke him from his nap. "Good morning, Mr. Ouwinga."

"Well, young man …." he replied with strength as he reached for his glasses. He must not have been too deep in sleep, I thought, and I suddenly wondered if he had been praying. "Good to see you again."

His tone assured me that I had done the right thing. I smiled at him. "Let me go get Teunis and we can visit for a while. That OK?"

"Well, that'd be great." The old man answered. "You go get that old wooden shoe."

And I was off across the room to wrestle Teunis Riemersma away from the boob tube. The three of us had just shared some small talk when Paul DeGraaf entered the doorway across the room. I was surprised to see that he was now consigned to using a walker and, unlike the other two, seemed to have aged considerably since I was last here.

Some of the fire remained in his voice, however. "Glory be ... if it ain't ... our favorite ... young garbio." His words came slowly, softly, yet deliberately as he worked himself down into one of the plush lounge chairs with the aid of Margie. "It's high time ... ya got back here. Where ya been ... keeping yourself?"

Feeling a sense of guilt, I apologized for my long absence, and I queried the three on their health, their children, and what they'd been up to. After I realized the silliness of that last question, I changed the subject to the bitter cold that had a grip on Chicagoland. That sent the men into recalling great cold snaps of years past. I politely listened and learned for several minutes. After an appropriate time and enough lessons on meteorology, I brought up the failing health of our mutual friend John Van Otten.

"They tell me that John's not too well." I opened.

"Yah, tis gettin' closer to te end for him," Riemersma noted, matter-of-factly. "He'll not be missin' his Harriet too long."

A moment or two of silence and reflection.

"Well, I'm sure ready to go," Ouwinga stated nonchalantly. "I don't know why the Lord don't take me one of these days."

Somewhat taken aback by his bluntness, I remained quiet for a time. I always knew him to be so composed and self-assured. A thought entered my mind. "Mr. DeGraaf, when you first came in the room, you called me a Garbio. I've always wondered. How do you spell that? Do you use an eo or io or ...?"

Riemersma jumped in, a little too quickly, "Hey, tat's easy. You spell it G A R B ... Hey, how do you spell tat? Jake, wat you tink? I never see it in print; te old guys just always used to say it; used to call all of us people 'garbios.'"

Ouwinga was eager to oblige. "Well, I think it's spelled G A R B I O, but I don't really know. I don't think you'll find it in a dictionary. And where it came from, I don't think anyone knows."

"Te Italians, tat's who," said Riemersma. "At least, tat's what I heard ... tat te Dagos from down on Fulton Street used to call te Dutchmen right off the boat by tat name. I tink tey was making fun of tem, what wit picking up the garbage and such. Tey tink tey were high an' mighty, cause tey got here a couple years before us."

"Well, I heard that story too, Teunis," Ouwinga admonished his friend, "but I don't know if we can say that it's true."

"It ... sounds true ... enough ... for me." DeGraaf added, laboriously. "I believe ... it."

"Tere—if Paul tinks it so, ten it's so."

From the adamant look on Riemersma's face and the exasperated expression on Ouwinga's, I figured it was time to change the subject.

"Mr. Ouwinga, Mr. DeGraaf, Mr. Riemersma" I asked, scanning the three visages one by one. "What happened with Mr. Van Otten's business? Why did he lose it?"

A pained expression came across both Ouwinga's and Riemersma's faces, while the countenance on DeGraaf's face became animated as he struggled to get out the words, "Da Mafia … guys came and … took it … is what happened. Dey would say … dey took it fair and square … but none of us … didn't dink so." The unexpected strain of his speaking caused the old man to cough several times, and Margie, sitting several tables away, came to determine what had prompted the old man to become so agitated. I glanced at her with an apologetic look as if to say that it was my fault. I mumbled something to the effect that it may have been the topic that I brought up. The warning look on her face reprimanded me sufficiently.

"Well, son. That's fine that you asked that question." Ouwinga said reassuringly, making me feel slightly better and causing our chaperone to retreat to her station. "What happened to John's business was public knowledge."

My eyes had widened with curiosity and the men could tell I wanted to know more. "And …?" I led off, fully expecting one of the three to fill in. I wasn't disappointed.

"Tey wanted to get in on te trash business," Riemersma began.

I interrupted, a little incredulous. "The Mob …? I thought they just did things like drugs and prostitution and gambling."

"Rough characters … dem guys." DeGraaf said, struggling to get it out.

"Ya … tey musta tought it was real easy to do," Riemersma went on, "just drive the truck down te road and te garbage just hops into te back. And ten tey go pick up te money."

"But why Van Otten"? I asked. "Why'd they pick on that poor guy?"

"Well, he wasn't the only one, young man." Ouwinga added. "There were others, not many, a few. Just unlucky, I guess. That, and the fact that his business was all on the north side."

"So?" I wondered. "What did they do? Just go up to Mr. Van Otten and the others and say they were taking over, like in the movies?"

"Well, no, of course not." Ouwinga answered. "He and the few others were followed for several nights. Stop by stop, building by building, we imagine. They must have taken notes; figured out which places they wanted the most, which stops looked the easiest. They did some bullying … one time especially. Then they went up to the customers and offered their services. That, along with a few dirty looks or implied meanings, and within a half a year, John, along with VanLonkhuyzen and VanLaar Disposals, went belly-up."

"Why ton't you tell him about when tey went after VanLaar in te 31st Street dump. Put him in a bind, tey tid. And ton't forget about Nick Vander Puy, Jake."

Riemersma reminded. "His business was cut in half."

"Well, you're right about that, Teunis. I had forgotten. All that stuff is good to forget."

"So then what?" I wondered. "The mob's not in garbage now; hasn't been as long as I can remember."

"Ah, yout' ...." Riemersma muttered.

"Well, it's nice to not know everything, young man." Ouwinga offered. "Like I said, they didn't know how hard the work really was, maintaining the trucks, the heat in the summer and the cold in the winter, the rats, the maggots ...."

"You said?" Riemersma interjected. "I'm te one who said it, Ouwinga!"

"That's right—you brought it up first. Go ahead, Dutchy," and Ouwinga cracked a smile. I sensed a joke in there somewhere.

"Ya done said it, Ouwinga. Tat and te fact tat tey couldn't find a lot of dumps to take teir trash."

"Why is that?" I asked.

The three men exchanged glances that almost could pass as smirks.

"Well," said Ouwinga, in an offhanded manner, "the fact that our people owned most of them might have has something to do with it. In any case, within two years the three men who were heading it up decided to bag it. It didn't have the glamour of some of the other things they often did."

"What about Van Otten's old stops then," I wondered. "And the other guys—weren't they able to get them back?"

"John tid get some of his business back," Riemersma explained, "but he never got up to te five routes he once had. Tose who knew him close, and I'll admit tat's not me, said he never was te same. Like he lost some of his fire. Can't blame him, kinda. And te other two, by tat time VanLaar and VanLonkhuyzen had moved to Michigan. Besides, Leddenga was starting to grow, gobbled tem up. Tem, and half of Nick's."

Both Ouwinga and DeGraaf nodded. I noticed Ouwinga looking at me intently. "So the Mafia tried garbage for a while." I mused. "Not a very glorious business for them to get into, was it? Specially when it's cold like this, huh?"

"Yah," Riemersma offered, "I tink tat's what tey tought, too!"

"So, Mr. Riemersma," I questioned, glancing out the window and changing the subject, "what did you hate worse—when it was really cold like this or the heat?"

"For me, no question—te heat. Garbage on te streets was a bear when it was 90°. No shade on tem streets, te maggots would be so many after a good rain. Ya get a lot of grass and stuff. No, I tidn't like te summer at all. Now te winter not tat bad on te homes. Some of my days would be pretty short. Not all tat yard waste. People just don't make much trash in winter, 'cept Christmas, of course. And ten we got good tips," he paused, "sometimes."

DeGraaf had been uncharacteristically quiet, and after closer examination, I saw he was almost asleep. I was sure he had an opinion on the subject, but figured that would have to wait for another day, or maybe never. Nevertheless, Ouwinga, who had always worked and operated his scavenger business in the city, had a different take.

"Well, Teunis, there might have been less house garbage in the winter out where you were, but it was a different story in the city. Our rigs couldn't get in and out of the streets and alleys after a big snowfall; cars would be stuck, sometimes abandoned, blocking our way. And lots of times, the trash would freeze solid right in the containers." Ouwinga continued, getting exasperated with the memories. "Crazy idiots would sometimes load wet slop in 10 degrees and expect us to be able to empty it the next morning. Awful frustrating when the driver raises the box and only half the stuff falls out, the rest stuck solid."

"What would you do?" I wondered.

"Well, the only thing we could do, aside from leaving the container sit in the garage overnight. The guy on the loader would have to scrape the box out, take twice as long to empty that way. So don't be thinking the winter was my favorite time."

Our discussion continued for a while, with good bantering going on between Riemersma and Ouwinga, and I just listening. DeGraaf was sound asleep by this time. In time the staff came through the lounge reminding all that lunch was ready. As Margie came to wheel Ouwinga to the dining room, he caught the two of us by surprise.

"Well, young man." He glanced at her, his usual mode of mobility, and then turned to me. "I was wondering if you could bring me to dinner."

"I'd be happy to," I quickly offered. With a reassuring look from Margie, I took hold of Ouwinga's wheelchair, leaving her to assist DeGraaf, who by now was just waking from his nap.

We were no more than ten feet out the door when Ouwinga asked me to sidetrack over to his room, saying that he had to retrieve something. As we rolled down the hallways, I sensed he had something on his mind. We had just entered his room—Number 126, South Wing—when he asked, "Well, friend, what are your plans for all the stories that you have been getting from us garbagemen over the years."

I admitted that I was keeping a journal and that someday I wanted to write a book on the topic.

"Well, then there is something that I should tell you, my friend, something that only a few people know."

I looked at the elderly gentleman, who I had been acquainted with for much of my life, and suddenly realized that there was more to him than I had thought. He eyed me with a serious expression and I could tell this was not about rats, accidents, or even his least favorite minister. I closed the door, sat heavily on his bed, and returned his look. "I don't know for sure what I will do with these tales you've shared with me, Mr. Ouwinga. However, if I ever put them down on paper, I would be very sensitive to people's names. I hope you realize that."

"Well, not that it matters much anymore. Soon all of us will be gone. Even now I think there are only three of us left who know what I'm going to tell you."

I remained silent; realizing there was nothing of value for me to add. What information that lay in that room was in Ouwinga's mind and, I hoped, was about to come out. I looked at his tired eyes, somewhat graying with age and wondered at all the things they had seen.

"Well, it's what we were talking about in the lounge a while ago. Remember John Van Otten losing his business to the mob."

I nodded.

"Well, you got to realize that it wasn't just John they went after. Like we said, VanLonkhuyzen, VanLaar, Vander Puy, one of the Boer boys, there were others too. Like Paul said—those guys could be some pretty rough sometimes."

"That's right," I recalled. "Mr. Riemersma said something about VanLaar and the dump. What was that about?"

"Those are bad memories, son. All of us felt real sorry for Ken VanLaar." I could see Ouwinga's emotions rising. "One of the nicer guys down there in the city. Why they picked on him I'll never know."

"Mr. Ouwinga, want a glass of water or something?" I got up off the bed.

"Thanks, young man."

The old man was trying to compose himself, and I figured a break in the conversation would be good. I disappeared into the bathroom and soon came out with a full glass. Offering it to him, he motioned that he didn't want it right then. I placed it on the dresser top next to him. He went on.

"Well, like I said, VanLaar was too nice … they must have figured he would be an easy target."

"Yes..?" I was getting a little impatient for the story to unfold.

"Well, two guys followed him out west to the dump one day. They waited till he was all the way in, probably watched him back up and getting ready to dump his truck. The one thug somehow must have got the bulldozer's attention; there was only one dozer often in those days. Well, according to VanLaar, while he was busy along side of his cab, dumping his load, the thug forced the operator to start heading for his rig. VanLaar had just about emptied his truck when he heard the dozer and thought that the guy just about to run him over. Guess they weren't going after him, just his truck.

"Well, he could do nothing at this point, just watch as the operator—the guy behind him must have had a gun to his back VanLaar figured—was forced to push the vehicle down the hill of garbage. Kept pushing it for 40, 50 feet, until it finally tipped over. Meanwhile, the other goon was standing up on top, laughing like anything. In ten seconds, it was all over. This was toward the end of the day, so not too many other guys were in the dump to see this, not that they could have or would have done anything."

Fascinated by the image of a bulldozer and a garbage truck in a wrestling match with the helpless owner watching, I looked out Ouwinga's window on to the clean, pure crystals of snow outside.

"Well, like I said, all of us had heard what happened to VanLaar. Knowing him like some of us did; and that it took him the whole next day to get the truck out, and two more to get it running again, this was hard stuff for us younger guys to take. Do you know that within two weeks, he and his family were packing up and going back to Michigan, his wife's home?"

Ouwinga hesitated. "The anger burned in us for a long time, young man. It began to consume us, turn us into not very nice people, with some not very nice thoughts. And finally, a few months later, one of us did something that was bad, real bad. He's lived with it," he paused, "He lived with it for a long time. But I think I can share it with you … and just you, mind you, so it don't disappear into nothingness soon, when I'm gone." I could see that he was troubled.

I didn't know which "Boer boys" Ouwinga was referring to, but I did remember Vander Puy and VanLaar, and I figured I could determine which VanLonkhuyzen he meant. I knew that two of the three men he mentioned had died long ago. I kept my thoughts to myself.

"Go on," I said. "That's what I'm here for."

"He killed a man," the old man blurted out, "using his bare hands … and a barrel … and the truck."

I could see hurt written across Ouwinga's face; a trace of wetness appeared at the corner of one eye. I averted my glance quickly to the pattern of the carpet. I had never seen him like this. The impact of what he had just said began to sink in. I remained mute.

Composing himself, he went on. "Well, some guys were coming around to threaten us, to keep us scared of them. Naturally we were all thinking about VanLaar again."

"Us? You keep saying us. Were you down there, in the city? " I asked.

"Do you think I always had my own business? Well, I didn't. I worked with Nick downtown for two years before venturing off on my own. I was down there with the others when the Mob started coming around. We were all a group. You know that, young man. Half of us were related to the other half, grew up with each other, went to school together."

"I know, Mr. Ouwinga. Go on. How'd it happen?"

"The man who did it … I'll not say his name … doesn't matter anyhow. The guilty one could have been any of us. The two goons had been hassling him for several nights, blocking his way in and out of alleys, laughing, mocking. Each of us had had the same treatment for several weeks. And we all had heard what they did to VanLaar."

It was hard for me to picture Jake Ouwinga, approaching eighty years of age and wheelchair-bound, a man I thought I had cased completely, to be part of the scene he was sharing.

He continued. "This is how the mafia guys did things then, to show us what it would be like if they really got mad, you know, or if we resisted, called the cops or something."

He finally reached for the glass of water on his dresser and took a sip. The old man paused a moment and closed his eyes as if going back to a scene he had played out repeatedly. I could hear the distant sounds of dishes being picked up and dining hall talk and life. This story he was relating seemed so surreal; it didn't belong in this time and place. Yet, from his flushed face and agonized voice, I could tell the pain and the tale were real.

After a few seconds Ouwinga continued, gaining strength and resoluteness as the story developed. He became calm again, very deliberative, almost methodical in his narrative.

"Well, he had been having a rough day. I'll call him Tom, to give him a name."

"Tom …." I repeated.

He continued, "Yes, Tom … Tom was not in the mood to be bothered, maybe he had been seething inside, anticipating—I don't know. But when the one guy met him at a stop and started in on him like he had previously … now Tom had been emptying one of those smaller barrels from years ago that some places used. Well, he suddenly wheeled and struck the guy in the side of the head with it—struck it hard … I mean … *real* hard.

"The thug was knocked to the ground. Tom said he could see the guy was just in the act of coming to his senses and going for his gun. He knew that it was either kill or be killed at that point. So Tom came down as hard as he could with the flat side of the barrel across the man's head, almost tearing off his face. With gut instincts kicking in—you realize Tom was not a fighting man—he picked the limp body up and literally flung him like a bag of trash into the hopper. He pulled the handle, the blade came down and did its thing, and in three seconds, the man was crushed behind four inches of steel and into a wall of garbage."

My eyes traversed the room, from floor to wall to window to the old man sitting before me, sharing his soul. I wondered at the deep secrets each person has, and the elderly even more so. Ouwinga pressed on.

"Seeing the gun lying on the ground, Tom knew that had to be gotten rid of as well, and he ran the cycle once more. As the blade opened up, the body fell down into the hopper again. Tom could see that he was not yet dead, not quite. He had no choice but to throw the gun in and run the blade again. Of course, the cycle takes several seconds, enough time for the man, maimed and bloody, to see and know what was occurring." Ouwinga paused. "Tom has lived with the sounds of that night and the last look on the man's face for a long time."

He stopped and looked me in the eye, and I tried to do the same. "I don't know what to say, Mr. Ouwinga." The dryness in my mouth was acute. "How have you and the other men been able to keep this inside?"

"With wives and kids, and positions in life that we were aiming for, we had to."

"Go on with the story, please." I replied. "It doesn't end there."

"Well, no, it doesn't. We don't know how long it took for the man to die. Tom drove off with the bloody mess in his truck. He needed to get the evidence soaked up and figured that within a few stops there would be enough trash to cover everything up. Apparently it was. In twenty minutes all the evidence of what had happened in that North Side alley was absorbed into the load."

I suddenly had a flashback. "Jake," I asked, "I recall a newspaper item from when I was a young kid. Where did 'Tom' take that load?"

"Where he had been taking most of his loads those years, to the incinerator in Cicero. Yes, you remember right. The charred remains were found, coming up one of the conveyer belts, but they didn't have enough to go on there." Calm was returning to Jake's face. "As far as the police could ever tell, it was some transient from any place in the city. No one ever reported somebody missing. The papers stated there was an official inquiry, but nothing ever came out of it."

"But Mr. Ouwinga, what did the Mob do?" I pressed. "They wouldn't take one of their guys getting killed without retaliation."

"Well, as near as we could figure, they never learned for sure what happened to him. That didn't stop them from getting what they were after—the trash business on the north side. Van Otten parked his trucks and went to work for somebody else. VanLaar and VanLonkhuyzen, like I said, were already packed up and went out of state, and Vander Puy resigned himself to running his two trucks out west. That's about the time I bought my first route, way out west and in the suburbs, out of their neighborhood."

I was about to interject something when he changed tone, sadness in his voice. "There was one mystery though, that those of us down there always wondered about. Three weeks later, Vander Puy's son was killed in a car accident. Cops at the scene said it looked like the young man—he was only eighteen and Nick's only boy, mind you—must have fallen asleep."

Ouwinga stopped and asked for that glass of water finally. I handed it to him and waited for the story to continue. He took a deep, refreshing drink and went on.

"His car went through a temporary barricade down at Wells Street and they found it, with him inside, at the bottom of the Chicago River. Was that a "getting back at us act" for one of their guys? Some of us always kind of wondered, but of course, there was nothing to do about it. And maybe you know, Vander Puy was never quite the same after that."

I looked at the clock on his desk, peering out from his collection of family photographs and memorabilia of his wife, who passed away thirteen years earlier. "Mr. Ouwinga, I need to get you to dinner before they close down."

"So, young man," he said, surprisingly cheerfully, as I rolled him down the hallway, "You've heard an earful today, I reckon. You going to remember all this?"

"Yes sir, Mr. Ouwinga. It'll be great fodder for my writing."

"Well, then," he cracked a sly smile. "I guess I'll have to kill you. We still got to keep these stories a secret."

"What?" I quickly recovered, with a grin on my lips as well, "kill me for writing about the cold in the winter and the heat in the summer?"

18
Relics

It has now been fifteen years and more since we left the Chicago area for Washington State, where clouds and towering firs, cedars and hemlocks are the predominate features, not flatlands and massive buildings, suburbia and landfills. However, it is always good to come back to where I was reared. Over the whine of the jet engines and through the whoosh of filtered atmosphere comes the pilot's voice from the cockpit.

"Pardon me, ladies and gentlemen. If you look on your right, you can catch a glimpse of the Mississippi River. We are just passing over Bettendorf, Davenport, Rock Island, and Moline, or as the locals call them, the Quad Cities. Expected arrival in the Chicago area is in approximately 55 minutes. We hope you have had a pleasant trip with us this time and look forward to serving you again in the future. Again, thank you for flying Southwest."

That is always my signal. I begin to look out the window soon after I pass the Mississippi River, scanning fruitlessly for the telltale bumps of a massive sanitary landfill in the landscape below. I never see what I search for but I know they exist; I put enough material in several to raise them a few inches.

This is what I envision from my seat high in the sky: a prominence upon the horizon, a singular large mound of earth that appears as an unusual formation. No forests or rivers, canyons or hills will accompany it; instead, I expect a few holdout farms and creeping suburbia surround it. The contributions of mine, combined with the tens of thousands of others over the years have created sanitary landfills that line the perimeter of the Chicago area, some of which reach hundreds of feet in elevation.

If I am lucky, I may observe that the landfill is still in the process of growth. Matchbox trucks would be laboring up its sides. At the center of their attention, I might see several queen-ant machines being fed this continual diet of waste. Yet, from the airplane we cannot smell the odors arising from this mound of refuse and floating over the nearby land. Passing over quickly, we would not note the thousands of trucks that come to this landfill day after day, queuing at the entrance before dawn and continuing their steady flow to closing time. I can imagine it though. Every time I arrive from the West by air, I search for one of the landfills, but I never see them.

Often, driving out of the airport, I find myself falling back into the habit of looking at passing garbage trucks. Moreover, not only the truck or the name of the company, but even into the cab. Was I thinking I would recognize the driver? I realize that not many other people have such tendencies. I try to keep it a secret.

Of course, I see no familiar faces, unlike years previously when I actually might recognize a friend or coworker. Even some of the types of garbage trucks appear unlike those I worked on. Criminy, I wonder, has the job changed that much that I couldn't even do it anymore?

Of course, the job has changed, I remind myself. All jobs change—indeed, all life changes. The waste business surely has. The fading technology of the first years when I worked on the truck was *innovative* back in the forties. Now trucks have rear vision cameras and onboard computers. The foul smelling environmental hazards we called dumps are no more; now the depositories of our refuse have become high tech, multi-layered, much-protected sealed vaults, still foul smelling, of course. The dark and brooding loading docks of yesteryear, haunts of many a transient and many a rat, seem to have all been replaced with brightly lit, security patrolled delivery zones. What would take two men a whole day to load onto a truck is now accomplished by one in a fraction of the time, but that one worker has to do it perhaps ten times today. Out with the old—in with the new.

There is change in the names as well. Whatever became of Metro, Arrow, Hoving, MidCity, Garden City, C & S, and Best, I wonder. Not only the names. The people, too. The old "Dutch Mafia" ...

The unfamiliar garbage haulers aside, it is good to be back again. Family and friends are doing well, if not a little older, some perhaps a little chubbier or balder. Yet, though my time is short, a call from a friend is enough to convince me to reserve a few hours to visit the old garbagemen at the Home. I learn that John Van Otten has passed on a few years back. That I expected. The word that Paul DeGraaf also has died from a heart attack takes me by surprise though. So, my first boss, and the man I knew since I was a little runt on Harvey Avenue ... both gone.

It was autumn weather, crisp and clear, when I arrived. Now, three days later, summer warmth has returned, clouds have gathered and the air has become heavy for what looks to be a powerful thunderstorm. I again hear the song of the cicadas. I sense that I haven't experienced this type of weather since I left years ago. I may yet get to see an old-fashioned thunder boomer before I leave, I hope.

When I arrive at the Holland Home for the Elderly after an absence of several years, it is obvious that, regardless of change that has occurred outside those walls, this remains so ... ethnic. Black and white photos of church buildings, school leaders and scenes of the old neighborhoods sprinkle the walls. The Dutch surnames still resonate with the endings of '*stra*, '*sma*, '*inga*, or beginning with '*Van*' and '*De*'.

I inquire at the desk for the location of Teunis Riemersma and Jake Ouwinga. After a cursory glance at me to determine my motive, the receptionist asks for my name and reason for visitation. I am spared the embarrassment of stating that I wanted to discuss old days on the garbage truck however. Before I get the words out of my lips, the woman clasps her hands together and remarks to all in the immediate area. "Why, Larry. I didn't recognize you. It's been years. Don't you remember me—Nancy Stob, now Keller?"

Dutch bingo, I think, but I lose this game. She doesn't look like the Nancy Stob I recall, but then again, that was thirty-two years ago. She goes on to remind me that I was one year ahead of her at school and that we were in some study halls together. After an interlude of reminiscing and laughter, seasoned with the awareness that—my, she looks old, and that I suppose I do too—I am on my way to visit the two men.

I cautiously approach Ouwinga's door. Years have passed since I last talked with this man. I worry—*will he remember me?* I recall his thick glasses—*will he still be able to see me? To hear me? To get out of bed? What if he is asleep? Do elderly people sleep all the time?*

I knock tentatively at his half open door and cautiously enter. To my relief, he is sitting at his table, eating a grapefruit, and appearing to be reading a magazine. "Hello, Mr. Ouwinga, how are you today?" I speak slowly. " ... ... Do you remember me?"

He glances my way through those same thick spectacles, takes a moment to let things register, I guess, and then softly smiles. He attempts a measured response, but halts, unsure.

I try to help him. "I'm Larry, and I used to visit with you years ago. I asked you questions about the garbage truck. Remember now?"

"Yes, I think I know you." He speaks softly, so softly I need to put my ear near his mouth. "Weren't you a teacher at the school?"

"Yes, Mr. Ouwinga." I grin. "Your memory is very good." I am surprised at his recollection, yet somewhat taken aback by the aged man before me. He is now nearly eighty-five years and showing it. His full head of white hair that I recall from previous visits has been replaced by a scraggily few. His face is thinning, his hands more bony; the veins protrude on his leathery looking skin. Mr. Ouwinga's body is failing him.

We chat lightly for several minutes as I labor to recall for him who I am and why I am here. I ask about his two daughters and the grandkids, how often he is able to get to church, what he thinks of the preacher (apparently a new one has come, though he admits that he rarely gets there), and how his health is holding up. As our visit wears on, he seems to perk up slightly, gaining in his ability to understand my conversation. Eventually I mention Riemersma.

"Mr. Ouwinga," I speak almost directly into his ear, "how is Teunis doing? Is he well? Would it be okay if we go to his room so we could visit for awhile?"

He looks at me and his eyes twinkle a little. "Well, yes, he is here all right," he replies, "still hanging on, ... like me ... although he isn't feeling very nimble lately. The weather probably, ... or his age. He's seventy-nine now." Ouwinga hesitates, as if to catch his breath. "Been looking it too. Looking ... acting. But let's go see him, he'll remember you, ... I think."

I grab his wheelchair to help him and learn that he is still able to maneuver his old body up and in. "Don't need your help, son," he gets out with some effort, and also with a certain air of the old Ouwinga pride, "but thank you for the offer."

We meander down the hallway slowly. Going by a window, I notice that the sky outside is turning dark. I take in the names again on the doors leading to each apartment and recall some that are familiar, but I also note many new. What is the average stay in this facility, I wonder? Yet some seem to thrive here. Jake Ouwinga has been here now for almost ten years. For others, it appears they lose spirit and pass on rather quickly.

Within a few moments, we arrive at Riemersma's residence; he apparently was moved to the assisted living section several months ago. He, like Ouwinga, is now confined to a wheelchair. He is facing the window, gazing out on the growing gray on the other side of the glass. I observe that the walls in his room have the usual eclectic grouping of photos and knick-knack found in senior housing. Each item seems to be a memento from some loved one or loved event in his long life. In the background, I hear a George Beverly Shea hymn.

"Hello, Mr. Riemersma." I say in a hushed tone, as I wheel Ouwinga in. I pause. He begins to turn my way. "Do you remember me?" I find myself speaking rather loudly. "My name is Larry. I've been gone a long time, but I'm back to visit with you."

His mind ... working in its inexorably slow way. Seconds in real time ... hours in appearance. A glimmer of sparkle in his tired orbs. A widening of his lips and his teeth appear.

"Ya ... I remember you .... I remember ... we talked about te garbage truck, tidn't we?" He attempts to sit up a little straighter and narrows his eyes in my direction.

"How's Teunis today, my friend?" Ouwinga says weakly. "Did you eat all your breakfast?"

"Sure tid, Jake." Riemersma is coming to life. He too pauses for a breath. "Margie—she make me. Says I a bad boy if I don't."

We chuckle and I wipe a small tear out of the corner of my eye. I suggest that we move to where there is more room. Soon the three of us are in the lounge where we often visited years ago. I see that the old Cicero plaque is no longer above the entrance to the room.

Situating ourselves in the same corner, I am about to begin some more small talk when Ouwinga surprises me. "So where are you … living now, son?"

"I live in Washington state," I answer, scanning the both of them, "far from here" … I picture where I am from …."Very far from here," I repeat.

"Well … I've been there … my wife and me … long time ago." Ouwinga says, in a muted voice, turning, and looking through his spectacles out the window, apparently seeing more than what is there. "Nice place. Lots of trees … trees and wide-open spaces …." He then turns back to me, "but this is your home …. you miss home?" I can still detect wisdom in his words.

"Yea, I do, lots of time." I respond, looking him in the eye. "That's why I come back often. But Washington's where my wife is from, so that's kind of home, too."

The wind begins to pick up now. A storm seems on the way. I glance out the windows and observe dead and dying leaves fighting to hang on. Many are losing the battle.

"Neber been tere." Riemersma softly volunteers. "Been to Iowa, t'ough. Tere and ten to Minnesota. Is tat like Washington?"

"No, not really." I answer. "Out there …

"How long you been gone, you say?" interrupts Ouwinga. Wisdom still interspersed with a touch of 'crotchetiness.'

"It's been fifteen years since I visited with you gentlemen." I answer, slowly and clearly, so they can both comprehend. "I've been back to see family and friends often. Just short visits, you know." I change the tone of the conversation. "I sure have noticed things changing here all the time. The city's getting busier, new suburbs sprouting up. … Mr. Ouwinga," I grab his hand to focus his attention on me. "Mr. Riemersma," I face him directly, "what has happened to all the old garbage companies? I've seen all new names on trucks since I've been here."

"Teir … almost all gone." Riemersma responds. "Hardly any left in te business … Jake and me … we're about te last … of te old association haulers alive."

"The who?"

"Teunis is using an old term … from a long time ago." Ouwinga explains. "you could say he just means … some of the old garbagemen."

"Well, yes, I understand that when one gets old, you get to retire and enjoy life. Get off the truck." I reply. "But what about the next generation? Why aren't the kids taking over?"

The words are just out of my mouth when I realize that I may have put my foot in it. I recall that Ouwinga had no sons, but that there were two daughters, and that one was divorced. I am clueless, however, as to what happened with American Disposal, his one-time thriving company. As for Riemersma, I know that he had his own route years ago, and that he sold it and went on to work for others.

Outside, I can hear the wind gathering in strength, ready for its onslaught with the rain.

Riemersma looks at Ouwinga. Ouwinga looks back. "Jake can … talk for himself," he begins weakly, then adds, with a grin, "he usually does. But I can tell you … tat it was hard for me … to keep my own route going … I just got tired of it. Every day … maybe six days a week … getting up in te dark. Ten coming home … do paperwork … make telephone calls. And ten … just when I tink I get some where … kablooey … truck breaks down. No, it isn't no fun … living life tat way."

Ouwinga seems content to let the man give his story without interruptions, and Riemersma continues. "Ten Browning Ferris came along … and offered … to buy me out and even … my old trucks … tey promised me good money … wit less headaches." He looks at me as if to receive forgiveness or understanding. "I couldn't say no. My two boys … I don't know … tey might have followed me... don't know if I wanted tem to." He turns to Ouwinga. "Was I wrong …?"

"No … no …." Ouwinga's answer is drawn out. He turns my way, not facing his friend.

"But now I just sit here," Riemersma continues " … wit all te time in te world, till I die … wish I had tings to do … or some ting to have headaches about."

I look at Ouwinga hesitantly. "What became of your company—American Disposal?"

"Well … I sold it … in pieces … when I knew my girls didn't want to be part of it." He coughs a raspy tone and I can tell this is hard on him physically. I signal the girl, and make a motion like I am taking a drink. She catches my drift, and gets up to go to the kitchen.

He continues, "Well … like Teunis said … it was getting tough … for me … regulations … too many rules … dumping … insurance. Some of us were sued for all … kinds of things …." He pauses. The attendant comes with three glasses of water and the men both take their fill. I sip mine. "My girls and their kids … I took care … of them. They don't have to work hard now …."

"And I'm sure they appreciate that, Mr. Ouwinga." I feel the two men need some measure of reassurance. "Your children love you very much."

Both men are silent for a while. I look outside. Although my direct view of the sky is blocked by an overhanging roofline, I can see the day turning a greenish hue. Many years have passed since I have seen this roiling and boiling of the atmosphere, and my inner little boy is eager for the storm to come. I wish I was out gazing at the clouds and not in this envelope they call a retirement home.

I am brought back to reality when Ouwinga catches me off guard. "I don't think so."

He looks me in the eye and then the two men glimpse each other. Riemersma nods and is about to open his mouth when a flash of brilliance in the sky shoots across the window. Wrestling with competing emotions, I put my arm on Ouwinga's shoulders as I think to myself that I haven't seen lightning like that for a while. Seconds later the crack of thunder reverberates through the center. My excitement at the impending weather is muted by the man's stark words.

"Why do you say that, Mr. Ouwinga?"

"I'm just an old man now … no use to any one … no place to go to … nothing to do … my girls—they don't visit me. That's what I want …. just someone to talk to … something to do … I want to get out … see something other than just shopping malls and museums." He peers out the window.

Outside the squall is beginning, with heavy drops landing on the sidewalk in a helter-skelter fashion. A germ of an idea begins to hatch in my head.

I turn to the men again. "Where do they live?"

They look at me blankly.

"Your family," I glance at Riemersma, "Your sons." I turn to Ouwinga, "Your girls. And both of you—you have grandkids." I repeat, wondering if the crazy thoughts in my mind will work, "Where do they live?"

"Mine live on … te Sout' side now …." Riemersma responds, "Orland Park, Palos … down around tere."

"Iowa," Ouwinga offers, " … and Michigan."

The rain is coming heavy now. I turn back to the view outside, entranced by nature's scene. The branches outside appear to hang on for dear life. Leaves of every color flutter and swirl inches outside the glass. The sidewalk is alive with bouncing bubbles. I stand up and move closer to the window, fascinated at what I see.

Ouwinga observes my interest. "It doesn't do this in Washington … does it?"

"No … I haven't seen this for years. I love it."

I realize that the men sense my pleasure in the storm. Silence is understood for the next several minutes, even as I formulate a plan that I am not convinced will work.

In time, Thor ceases his thundering and the tempest is over. Now I have the desire to help these old men *feel again the wind and rain of their life.*

"Gentlemen," I turn to look at them both. "I've got an idea." I move close to the two, as they sit side by side in their wheelchairs. I again gently grab their hands. "How about if I take you out of this warehouse for the dying one of these days. And I won't take you to some mall or to the library or some museum. I want to take you where you left your life's work. We'll go visit some of the old landfills that you often went to, to see if they still are operating, and to see the trucks still coming in to dump. And maybe I can track down one of your old trucks, just so's you can get that feel again, maybe even crawl in to the cab."

Their eyes widen and Ouwinga starts to open his mouth as if to say something, and then hesitates.

I continue talking at a rapid pace. "Mr. Ouwinga, you may not have your trucks and your company anymore, and Mr. Riemersma, the company you worked for is long gone. Most of the men you worked with are gone as well. However, the landfills are still there. At least some of them."

Neither responds right away, and I don't know if what I am suggesting registers in their minds. The storm outside is beginning to abate a little. I continue. "I know it's not regular, not the norm for people to visit dumps or look fondly upon old garbage trucks. Heck, we might be the only visitors to go to the landfill this year."

I see doubt and disagreement in their faces, so I try a different tack. "And I know it might not be easy for the three of us to get in. However, Mr. Ouwinga, with your connections from a long time ago, I bet with a few calls, it'll happen. Right?"

He takes the bait and seems energized by the idea. "Well, now I do suppose I could call my nephew …."

Riemersma appears to resist, "But what will te people here say if we …."

Ouwinga rises to the occasion. "Who cares … what they say, Teunis? Who are they anyway? Besides, we're big boys now … right?" He coughs, and then clears his throat. "We can go where we want."

Riemersma's features betray a growing grin and his eyes, weak as they are, sparkle. The weather outside or my proposal seems to be stirring his spirit. "Ya … I guess I can still go out into te world now … If you just help me into te … wait a minute." He has a worried look on his face. "How we gonna get in a car … and up tose hills? You got two old cripples here … young man … in wheelchairs."

"Don't worry about that, Mr. Riemersma. I can get a van that will have more than enough room. Better yet, I'll get one of those SUVs. That will be perfect."

It seems I have Ouwinga convinced already. "Well, … I think it will work … I bet I can get John Aardema to help us … he could pull some strings for us."

Riemersma beams like he's fifteen years younger. "Oh, ya … Aardema could make a few calls … tat I ton't doubt." He peers at me and then looks at the dying storm outside. "It's been a long time since I was far away from tis place … and it's been a long, long time since I been near a truck or at a dump." His visage suddenly darkens. "Larry, I tink teir all closed."

"So what, if we know who to get a hold of, someone will open a gate or two." I continue, even as I begin to see some problems. I again grab the two men's hands and look them square in the face. "Listen, I'm going back home to Washington later today. However, I'm coming back in November. If you men promise to stay healthy, I'll arrange with the director here for you to escape from this place for a day." Their wrinkled faces break into broad smiles. "I'll get a vehicle and I'll be in contact with you."

I look at their tired eyes and bony hands, and waver a second. Am I crazy to be doing this? Can I convince the director? More importantly, can I convince their children? I look out the window and see the clouds breaking up. The storm that so recently was thrashing the trees with pent-up energy is gone. This is most likely the last downpour before winter.

I turn again to the two old scavengers. "Mr. Riemersma … Mr. Ouwinga … are you up for this adventure?"

Their enthused "*yes*" in unison is still in my ears as I board the airplane and head for the West Coast. I will begin arrangements the next day.

19

Legacy

The Internet is a marvelous tool for locating goods to purchase, people to email, and even used, but still functioning garbage trucks. Acquiring the vehicle identification numbers from one of Ouwinga's old vehicles is the hardest part, but once that is determined, I am delighted and surprised to find that one old American Disposal rig is still in use in a small town just over the Wisconsin border. A few phone calls and a very understanding garage foreman allows me to set the date.

It is a dry November Saturday, and the three of us are in a van heading north on US 12, through the ever-spreading Chicago suburbs and out into the farmland. We see corn and soybean combines stirring up their clouds of dust. The smell of good farm production fills the air. Our objective, Pell Lake, is a nondescript little settlement perched astride an equally unremarkable body of water. The men in the ramshackle Quonset hut that serves as their garage look at me with suspicion, but that turns to acceptance when they see my companions. As I labor to get Ouwinga and Riemersma out of our vehicle and into their wheelchairs, the man who I had communicated with earlier comes to his senses and realizing the moment, begins to help. The four of us, followed at a distance by five sturdy, coarse young men, grinning and wondering, bounce over the rutted gravel backyard of Pell Lake Auto Body and Truck service. There, in the back lot of a little town far from where the man labored for years, Ouwinga sees his old #43, a 25-yard Leach packer with an oversize hopper. The paint job applied to the truck has failed to obliterate the original markings and we can make out the faded lettering and numbering. The former president, part-time mechanic, and driver of American Disposal gazes at the hulking metal monster, now apparently even too shabby an item for the Pell Lake people to use. It sits enveloped by a bed of weeds, its windows history, tires cracked and sinking into the ground. Two small trees have sprouted in the hopper, where once thousand of tons of refuse had been carted off. Riemersma and I, along with the others, say a few words to Ouwinga, but he does not respond. His thoughts are somewhere and I know not if this has been meaningful or meaningless. Within ten minutes, we are again on the highway, heading homeward.

Ninety minutes later, we are at a park-like setting observing a soccer game in progress. The moms and dads roam the sidelines incessantly, throwing out warnings and urgings in rapid staccato fashion—"Get the ball, Go! Go!"

"Yea, thata girl."

"Susan, watch behind you!"

"Patty, cross it over, cross it!"

"Kick it, Sara, now!"

The field on which the little bodies scurry back and forth is at the foot of an incline reaching perhaps 200 feet in elevation. Two wooden rails, separated by a 100-foot span, work their way up the top where they merge to form a semi-circle. Vegetation lines the periphery, leaving the center open, giving the appearance of a hay field on the rise.

"According to the map," I point out as best I can to the two men sitting in my car, "this little hill is the old North side landfill that Sexton opened back in the 1950s, his first of many. Now remember, Mr. Ouwinga and Mr. Riemersma, the county made a park out of it, for the kids to run up and down on, and sled in the winter, so we can't see it very well. However, if you take away the trees and bushes, you can make out the elevation rise."

They both nod their heads in silence.

"Just think … You men brought your trucks up here often, didn't you?"

"I never dumped here … ever." Riemersma clarified. "Too far nort."

"Well … I did." Ouwinga expressed quietly. "So different..."

"Yes, Mr. Ouwinga. I'm sure it is. Just like the others we've been to, isn't it? They make these old landfills pretty nice … cover 'em up so that no one knows what used to be here."

"Still here." He corrects me, with a smile.

"I stand corrected. You're right. What you put here long time ago—it is still here, isn't it? Well, at least some of it. But a lot of it is dissolved and rotted, right?" I get preachy. "Returned to dust and all that stuff, like it says in the Bible?"

After several moments, Ouwinga admits, in a thoughtful tone, "I put a lot of stuff in the ground here … that isn't going to rot. I'm glad … county … covered it all up. They did a good job …." The old man looks around expressively. I try to imagine the multitude of times he arrived here with his truck to empty a day's work.

"But we've been here long enough." I remind them. "Now it's time to go out to Greenville. They are expecting us soon."

* * *

Eighty minutes later, we find ourselves thirty miles west, at the summit of Greenville Reclamation Project, the Chicago area's largest sanitary landfill. The view from the top is indeed impressive. In a land without hills, this massive mound gives a unique perspective. Far on the horizon to the east emerges the skyline of the city, with the Sears Tower and the Hancock looming majestically over the others. To the north, west, and south, a nondescript view carries on and on, gradually disappearing as it merges with the cloudy sky. Buildings wide and narrow, long and short, of various colors and shapes, rise as if randomly planted by some giant farmer sowing seeds of concrete, brick, steel, and glass. In between there are intermittent expanses of green, lined by ribbons of gray going in all directions. A million-dollar vista, I think, and a shame so few people get to see this.

The three of us relax comfortably in the Suburban for a full thirty minutes, while the two men take turns recalling days past. Neither has been here since the 1960s, when this landfill was just started, then a cavernous hole in the Illinois prairie. Now it is almost abandoned, months before it is to be officially closed. However, through Ouwinga's name and some networking we have permission to be up here.

The occasional truck still comes lumbering up the gravel/rock road to dispense of its load, but by now the costs have become prohibitive to all but only the nearest disposal firms. Now it is just a shadow of its former self, eerily quiet, almost forsaken.

The wind begins to blow; scattering bits of plastic and torn fragments of paper in tight loops and swirls so that they never seem to land. Birds numbering in the hundreds, mostly seagulls, fly about, picking at the ground, while others seem content to swarm in circles, as if waiting for something better to come along, their call permeating the air. A fine dust is settling on the hood of my vehicle. Twenty yards to my left, I see what appears to be a large rubber boot protruding through the dirt. Off to my right, I notice a section of carpeting that wants to escape this landfill grave.

The air is heavy with rot, a permeating smell of decay and moldering vegetation. The daily covering of new soil tries mightily to conceal the odor; yet it is, for the most part, unsuccessful. The two men know this air and do not complain.

I look at Ouwinga sitting next to me, and then to Riemersma in the back seat. They are amazing old men and have seen much in their lifetime. I see, in them, the many who came before and have gone away. I recall Van Otten, who trained me, and DeGraaf, who showed me how to have fun.

But it wasn't all fun. I know it was hard for Riemersma and his family. I'd heard stories. Dutch immigrants after the First World War—couldn't do the English thing well—not many options open to him.

And Ouwinga and all his money—did he sacrifice as well, I wonder? His uncles and aunts moved to the heartland of Iowa when his father came to Chicago. He talked about his country cousins on occasion. He once shared that they scorned his city lifestyle and questioned his spiritual commitment.

I ponder. Is it easier to raise a family on the farm than in the city? One can be sheltered somewhat in the Heartland with corn and space all around and not people. God knows these four and the others tried, but they weren't always successful. Rumors have it that Riemersma's boys are worldly. Van Otten lost a boy in alcoholism, but he never liked to talk about it. A drink was always there for the garbageman as he worked his rounds in the city at night. So were women. And slippery money. Temptations abounded. Their churches, their neighborhoods, their schools, their families were *their Heartland* to flee to after work.

The two still with me banter softly and I just listen. As weak as their voices are, I hear of favorite trucks, crazy workers, and crazier happenings.

Ouwinga begins to chuckle and a broad grin breaks out on his old face. "What's so funny, Mr. Ouwinga? Thinking of something that happened here?"

" .... just remembering a driver … long time ago. Name was Moose … don't know why … he wasn't that big. Can't remember his real name … he was just … Moose." He coughs, every word an effort. I produce a cup of water and offer it to him.

" … he always liked to complain … make jokes … that his job didn't make sense."

He pauses and looks at me. "What did he mean, Mr. Ouwinga, saying it didn't make sense?"

He chuckles again. " … this was when I was working … for Dad … up north. I'd hear him grumble … you know, at the end of the day … ready to head for the dump. He'd say, 'Ya know, Jake, this job don't make no sense … we rush all day to fill up this here truck, then rush … to empty it.' Same joke … almost every day."

Ouwinga smiles again and has a far off look in his aging eyes. Riemersma is quiet.

"Did it make sense, Mr. Ouwinga?" I look at him and then to Riemersma.

Both men's faces are fixed onto one solitary truck ascending the long steep grade. They appear transfixed, their eyes widen. They see thousands of vehicles climbing with the one. All makes and sizes and every conveyance they have seen and heard join in their memories. They envision old Reos and Diamond Ts, Hendricksons and Reliables, along with the newer Internationals and Macks. They see Heil packers and Leach packers and even old Garwoods. The ancient garbagemen visualize the first rigs they worked and the latest container truck purchased, old dumpers and newer push outs; and, harkening back when they were young, the open tops in which men would tamp down the refuse with their weight as they wrestled trash barrels from back to front.

I take them out of their stupor "Mr. Ouwinga and Mr. Riemersma, if you could do your life over again, would you change?"

Ouwinga, feisty for an octogenarian, turns the question back to me. "Change—change what …? my name …? my religion …? where I lived …? The woman … I married?"

I am somewhat flustered, " … the occupation you chose to get into, Mr. Ouwinga …. garbage-hauling ...the hard work, the smell, the early hours, the …."

Weak as he seems, he still is able to interrupt. "Yes, what else … was so bad about the job?" He is smiling now, and I am squirming; yet, I plunge ahead, trying mightily to stay afloat in his sea of taciturnity. "I don't know. That is what I want to learn. Would you choose to do that line of work again, or knowing what you know now, go off to college and get into some other vocation?"

"Well … I never had much choice … going into a profession … was … as realistic for me as going into space … was for you. People did it … but we never knew them … never rubbed shoulders with them."

Riemersma nods in agreement and is about to add his opinion, but Ouwinga isn't about to stop. For a man in such an advanced age, he is remarkable in spirit. "But … there were worse jobs … everyday I knew that I had done a good day's work. I never cheated anybody … … I was giving a service … that people needed, wanted." Ouwinga gets a little too animated and begins to cough.

" … Watch next time there is a garbage strike ... Teunis, how come … you're so quiet?"

Before Riemersma can join in, I try to settle the man down. "Now, don't get too excited, Mr. Ouwinga. Remember, I am writing a book about the garbage truck and I just want to get your opinions." His countenance changes and a smile again graces his old features.

Riemersma has been looking for an opening. "Maybe you have te wrong idea … about te garbage truck, young man. It wasn't like a chain gang. We enjoyed te outdoors and tat was nice. It was always good to find tings …. was healthy job too, if you didn't get your arm chopped off..." Noticing my left hand, he quickly adds, "or your fingers … wait! … tat's right, wat I telling you tis for? You worked on … truck."

"Exactly," I smile, "But some people leave great monuments when they pass on. Architects design buildings. Statesmen leave treaties, politicians make laws, and inventors come up with ideas so that we can continue to use their gizmos or their whatjamacallits long after their gone. With all of our work, what monuments have we left behind?"

Silence ensues. It is a cold gray day outside. Fine particles of matter hang in the air. A majestic panorama spreads out over the horizon before the three of us, even as we sit atop a mountain of refuse. Transcendental thoughts. We watch the lone garbageman, oblivious of us, empty his load, going through his motions.

A short time of silence.

Riemersma breaks the quiet. "Some people do have teir monuments … as you call 'em. Some get great chances to do tings and … tey do 'em. Teir te chosen ones, by God …." He speaks slowly, deliberately, " … not all us so lucky. You can go crazy … tinking what if?"

Ouwinga remains mute. His face betrays emotion just below the surface. We continue to observe the man hundreds of yards distant. He appears an apparition among the windblown particles of dirt, scraps of debris and the ever-circling swarms of seagulls.

Riemersma reasons, "Just living to tis age is my monument … tat's what I'm tankful for."

Another moment of stillness.

Ouwinga speaks in a soft murmur, "Well, monuments don't always last … buildings get torn down … laws overturned … treaties forgotten... new inventions come … replace the old." He smiles at the two of us. "Maybe this hill … is as much a monument that we can expect …. it will be here for a long time."

Riemersma, the aged garbio, turns to his colleague, a question mark on his brow. "Jake …."

Ouwinga looks his way briefly, and then turns his gaze back to the truck or the man, I cannot tell which.

"Do ya tink tere's garbage in heaven?"

No answer from Ouwinga—no response—no further talking, just the wind swirling around our eyes.

The driver lifts himself back into the truck and begins the slow trip down to the highway beyond. Soon the vehicle and its accompanying cloud of dust fade away below the horizon. We are alone again. I would like to remain here for a spell. I know they do, as well. But they are very old and it is time for them to go home.

Postscript

Rear-end loading packer, roll-off boxes, dumpsters, and landfills—these are all terms with which the average American is unfamiliar. The development of the packing giant Leach 25-2R, along with the Dempster Dumpster, Heil Huge Haul, and other brands of roll-off containers revolutionized the waste disposal business. The Leach Corporation demonstrated its 25-2R (25 greatly compacted yards of trash in a body of hardened steel with a 2-yard loading area or hopper in the rear of the truck) as being capable of compacting a Volkswagen Beetle. For years it was the standard of the industry.

Packer Truck

Rolloff Truck

In an alternative to refuse pickup, the Dumpster and Huge Haul containers satisfied the need for the removal of larger and more unwieldy items, such as construction material, appliances, beams, i.e. anything too large for one man to handle. Introduced in the 1940s and 1950s and spreading across the industry and nation since, these innovations led to greater efficiency for waste management companies and more convenience for the average consumer.

Although sizes, capacities, engineering, and methods of removal vary, the basic principle is the same. What is essentially a steel box, ranging from as small as one cubic yard to as great as seventy-five, is filled with the customer's refuse. Smaller containers, of course, fit in hallways, garages, and any spot where cans and barrels of yesteryear called home. The larger units are located in alleyways, parking lots, and underground loading docks, in essence any location solid enough to withstand the weight. Roll-off containers have even been positioned several stories high.

No longer do the workers have to wrestle with the cans, drums, and the 55-gallon barrels, the back-breakers of earlier days. In theory, the hydraulic system of the truck does the work and the worker guides the process. Theories don't always cut it on the streets and in the alleys, of course. The smaller dumpsters can be brutally heavy to pull or push to the waiting truck. Snow or mud can make matters worse. And rubbish does not always pour out of the box like water. Items get jammed. Wet rubbish freezes on cold days. Customers have even been known to pour wet concrete into containers and expect the garbageman to make it disappear.

* * *

Of course, the trash we create does not simply disappear. It all must be either recycled or placed in the ground. By the mid twentieth century, the old garbage dump was replaced with the sanitary landfill. These landfills have been the focus of great innovation as well as controversy. Dumps were literally where the early trash collectors would deposit the garbage, which would be set afire and become a place for rats and wildlife to forage. Now the landfills are strictly controlled and, in essence, sealed off depositories of our waste, and indicators of our society's wealth. What will future generation archeologists think, and what will they find, when they probe these landfills?

Chicago

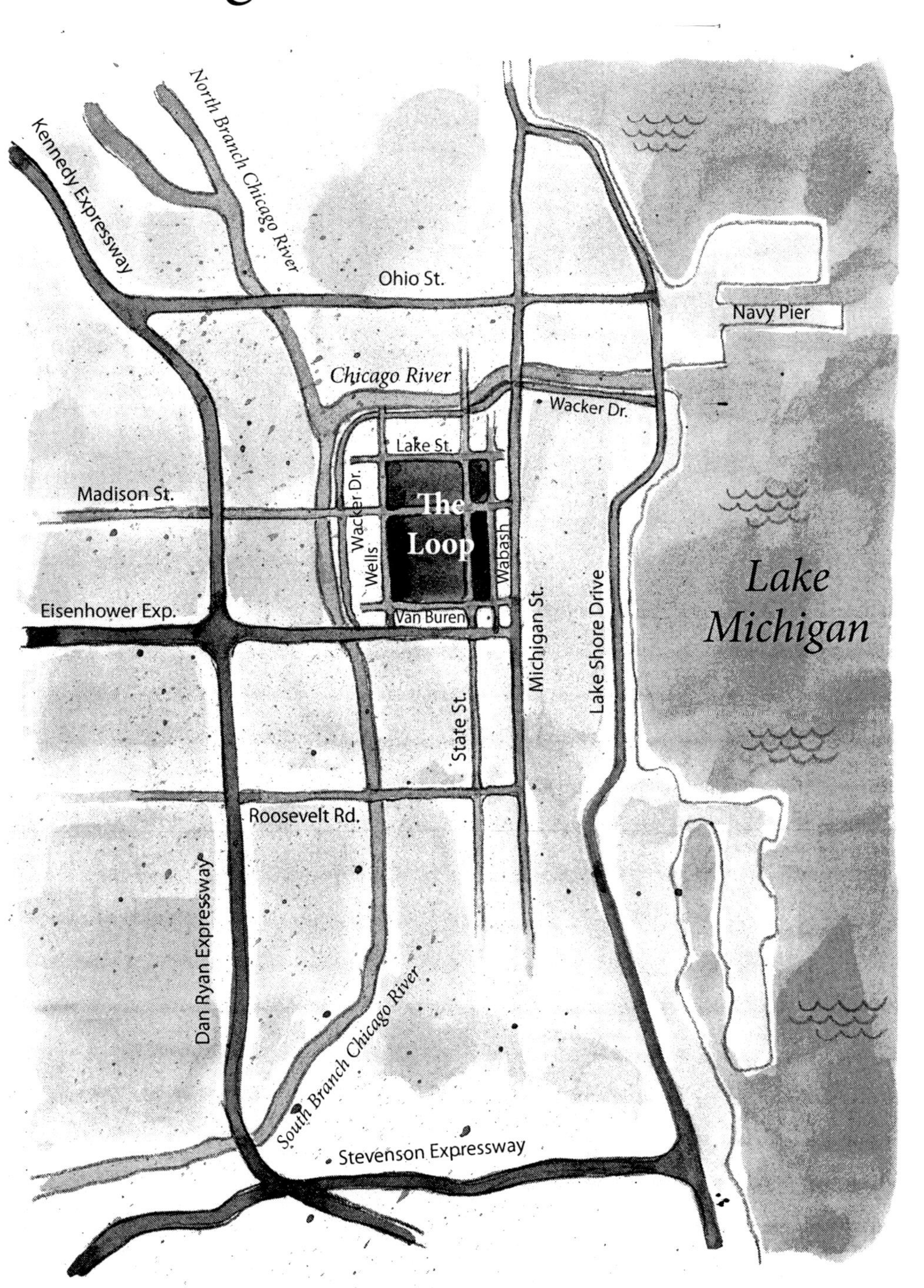

Kennedy Expressway
North Branch Chicago River
Ohio St.
Navy Pier
Chicago River
Wacker Dr.
Lake St.
Madison St.
Wacker Dr.
The Loop
Wells
Wabash
Lake Michigan
Eisenhower Exp.
Van Buren
Michigan St.
Lake Shore Drive
State St.
Roosevelt Rd.
Dan Ryan Expressway
South Branch Chicago River
Stevenson Expressway